"A SHOCKER!"
—Saturday Review Syndicate

Mirror, Mirror, on the Wall

is the story of a man driven by nightmarish glimpses of erotic horrors to a journey into his sexual past to escape that nightmare. But the nightmare is real and for Peter Hibben there is no chance of escape.

MIRROR, MIRROR, ON THE WALL is a story of sexual murders revealed in madness. It will horrify—*and haunt you.*

"Dazzling . . . a smash ending."
—San Francisco Chronicle

"Will keep you glued to the chair."
—Hartford Courant

Mirror Mirror on the Wall

BY

Stanley Ellin

A DELL BOOK

to Ms. Jeanne
Michael
Ellin

Published by
DELL PUBLISHING CO., INC.
1 Dag Hammarskjold Plaza
New York, New York 10017

I HAD BEEN WARNED about an incipient ulcer.

Right there, the insurance doctor had said, tapping me right there. Duodenal. Tensions work on it like sandpaper. Ease up.

So I am not surprised now to suddenly feel the pangs right there, as if all the bile in my digestive tract has been drawn into a syringe and injected into that one vulnerable spot.

But just how the hell does anyone ease up with this unexpected stench of gunpowder in his bathroom? And this sight of a large, fleshy, terrifyingly lifeless woman on the floor, apparently shot to death by the gun lying beside her?

My gun.

God almighty.

Carmina Burana is on the recorder in the living room, supplying background music by Carl Orff for my horrors. A chorus celebrating the pleasures offered by the living bodies of large, fleshy women raise mugs of beer and bellow a response to the tenor.

Poor Carl Orff. Too Nazified for my then wife, the former Joan Barash, daughter of Julius Barash of Barash Cleaners and Dyers at Broadway and 90th Street, One Day Service Our Specialty.

Remember that cute little scene? Remember her with her hands over her outraged ears? "Peter, please turn that goddam thing off."

"Are you blaming him for Dachau? He's a composer. He didn't kill any Jews."

"I know. Just turn it off."

"You know you're overreacting."

"That's my Semitic privilege. Now turn it off, or I'll kick that machine right in its electronic guts."

I turned it off. "Sometimes I wonder why the hell you married a *shegetz* to start with."

"Because you used to screw good."

Unforgiving little bitch. And that wasn't why. It was because she wanted to produce a *shegetz* all her own. A big, tough blue-eyed blond like Daddy Peter. Interior by Moses Maimonides. Exterior, courtesy of Peter Hibben.

And she had done it too. Produced Nicholas, exactly the son called for. And then would have devoured him, Yiddisher Mamma style, if it weren't for Daddy's watchful presence.

"Olim lacus colueran," sings the tenor.

"That's enough!" I command. "Shut up!"

Instant, ear-ringing silence.

Unnatural silence inside the house and out.

Now if that body and that gun could only be gotten rid of by the same magic.

I RECOGNIZE THE GUN. I do not recognize the woman.

Yet, trembling, sweaty, nauseating logic tells me that since the lady's remains repose on my bathroom floor in my own locked, barred, closed-circuit-TV-guarded apartment on Sheridan Square in Greenwich Village, and since she is semi-clothed in a way that makes it clear she had not simply stepped in off the street, there could have been some connection between us.

With emphasis on the physical.

Because she is a big, white-skinned, dark-haired wench, the coal-black hair shoulder length, the eyes exotically rimmed in black, the lips drawn back over clenched teeth and outlined in pale pink, the body garbed in unabashed Belle Époque whorehouse, a black lace brassiere with the center of each cup cut away to expose rouged nipples, a black garter belt clipped to black network stockings, black slippers with five-inch spiked heels—my God, when had that kind of footwear last been shown in shop windows—and over all a black chiffon negligee.

Black, pink and white. The face a geisha-white. The thighs, under the shadowy negligee, a glimmering paleness. And red. That is the blood trickling down the simulated mother-of-pearl laundry hamper, puddling on the tiled floor. And is that an ooze of it gathering at a corner of the slack mouth and starting to work its way down the jaw? It is.

Her position suggests she was caught at her prayers

when the bullet hit her. The hamper is pulled away from the wall, she is on her knees before it, her head resting sideways on it, her eyes glassily fixed on the full-length mirror attached to the bathroom door. Her arms dangle on each side of the hamper, fingers curled a little.

Caught at her prayers. No, ordered to them. Nympho, haste thee to thy orisons. She might have circumvented the closed-circuit TV, made her entrance, demanded I gratify her. That I get between those stout thighs and fill her to the brim. Eyes half closed, lips moist and parted, she pleaded.

Tempted, I refused to play ball. Explained that I had a schedule which didn't permit any such fiddle-faddle. For some reason, I had phoned in a gigantic grocery order to Gristede's and it was to be delivered any moment now. And the McManus & Nash offices were headed off in opposite directions again. There would be phone calls from McManus here in town and from Nash in London, and a lot of diplomacy to exercise. A pair of publishers can demand a great deal of diplomacy, especially when they each hold an equal share in the same business and hate each other across the Atlantic twenty-four hours a day.

And as company diplomat—she could understand that, I hoped—as the one essential agent through whom Charles McManus and Henry Nash would communicate with each other, I can hardly risk missing an emergency call from headquarters because I am under the sheets with her.

And Vince Kenna is up in arms again. Vincent Kenna, with the book clubs waiting to snap up his latest masterpiece. Six hits in a row. Six best-selling blockbusters. Six record-breaking paperback sales. It was Vincent Kenna who had to be catered to, not some strumpet looking to move in on Pete Hibben.

Joan refused to understand this whenever it came up.

"That was a hell of a thing. Invite him home for dinner at seven-thirty, then you show up at eleven."

"What about it? I phoned from the office, didn't I? I told you I'd be late."

"You sure did. And as soon as bright-eyes got the idea, he really went to work on me. I am telling you the exact and literal truth, Pete. He damn near had his hand in my pants before I could convince him he was just good old Uncle Vince in this house, and nothing more."

"All right, so you obviously did convince him."

She stared at me. She shook her head. She whispered it. "You know something? You really, honest to God sound as if you wanted me to go to bed with him."

"Now look, Joan—"

"You did want that! And I never even realized it until just now. My God, I didn't even believe it when I just said it. But I do now. It's one of the things that's been scaring me so much. Only I never let it come to the top of my mind where I could get a good look at it."

"Joan—!"

"It's true, isn't it? You want Vince to crawl into bed with me. It would make him so happy. It would solve so many things for us!"

I slapped her. For the first time in our married life, I played that trump card, muscle. The worst part of it—although also the luckiest—was that I slammed my hand against her cheek, not with unrestrained fury, but with controlled force; if I had let go completely, I might have knocked her head right off her shoulders. The bad part was that I was so obviously not acting out of blind, uncontrollable—hence excusable—rage, but was physically punishing her for being a naughty, big-mouthed little girl.

It hurt. She pressed a hand against the flaming red patch on her cheek. "Is that all," she said, "or is there more coming?"

"Joanie, I didn't mean to do it! I don't know what got into me!"

That damn capacity for identifying with the other

person. For being the other person. In this immediate
case my wife, small, defenseless, fragile despite those
over-sized breasts, confronting the big male hulk that
towered frighteningly over her. Undoubtedly, it was
those breasts which had flagged Vince Kenna into
lowering his head and charging. Strictly a breast man,
Vince. Eye-bulgingly, obsessively so. Had he known
little Mrs. Hibben before her pregnancy, he wouldn't
have flicked an eye at her. Then, miraculously, the
pregnant Mrs. Hibben's boyish upper structure had
blossomed. From lemons to oranges to cantaloupes.
No more rubbing creams, no more of those elbow-wav-
ing exercises which made her look like a chicken fu-
tilely straining to take wing. Cantaloupes, by God.
And after Nick was born, after she went back to
featherweight, the cantaloupes remained.

She could have wept for joy about it. Until Vince
Kenna, that gray-haired, twitching-fingered, best-selling
melon fancier came long.

I shared her feelings now, guiltily knowing her pain
and impotent anger. Until she said, "If you're going to
beat me up, shouldn't I bring Nick down to watch? It
ought to make him so proud of his big strong
daddy."

So she was not going to forgive me. She never did.
She recorded each sin in an account book and could
tell the balance at a moment's notice.

I thought we had been having this out in our bedroom; I suddenly realize we are not. We are in the
living room, and she's opening a drawer of the desk,
hauling out that massive account book. She looks
around for a pen, finds a suitable one. "This is really
a red-ink job," she says. "All capitals. And italics."

And somehow, frighteningly, there is Irwin Gold
making himself part of this.

Very frighteningly.

Because Joan and I had that vicious little confrontation about Vince Kenna three years ago. She
didn't even know of Irwin Gold's existence then. He

didn't step into the picture until a year later, when he was nominated by her family to handle her divorce from me.

Irwin Gold. Brass in the daylight when he cooked up corporation contracts, gold at night when he presided at Civil Liberties Union meetings. Wiry little bastard, all sideburns, sympathy, and shit. He oozed sympathy. For Joan, for Nick, even for me. Oozed it all over the skids under Joan, so that six months after she got the divorce papers in Juarez she slid into marriage with him, never even suspecting how she had been conned. That was the gut-wrenching part of it. He sympathized with me so much before, during, and after the divorce that Joan knew she had someone to share her belated anxiety for me. Her own occasional grudging sympathy. Share it with him at dinner, at the theater, and right through bedtime afterwards. They probably panted out their sympathy for me in chorus while he was all over her in bed.

Pure Gold. Letting me have every weekend with Nick even when Joan pulled up short at the idea. *Come on, sweetie pie, the big slob is nuts about his son. Give him a break.*

"What do you call him?" I bluntly asked Nick. "Uncle Irwin?"

"Nope. He said just call him Irwin. So I do."

"You get along with him all right?"

"Most of the time. He tries, so I try. He wants to be buddies, I make like a buddy. It's not always easy."

"You mean he pushes too hard."

"Uh-huh. Mostly it shows up in games. Like we're playing Monopoly with Grandma and Grandpa, and Irwin is doing a lot of kidding around and laughing, but I know he'd cut everybody's throat to win. Same in tennis."

"You play tennis with him?"

"Uh-huh."

"He play a good game?"

"He calls it a smart game. Dinks, lobs, rabbit turd.

You could take him love set every time out."

"I get the feeling you could, too."

Nick gave me a big heave of the shoulders. "Maybe. But I don't."

"You throw him games?"

"He dies when he loses. He puts on the smile and the big handshake, but he's dying inside. Like he's not a bad guy really, only he's got to win or he dies. It's the nature of the beast. So sometimes I let him win."

This, mind you, from a fifteen-year-old kid.

And, weirdly, here is Irwin Gold on the scene right now, while Joan is paying me off for Vince Kenna long before she had even met her shyster. Intimately on the scene, because we are somehow in my bathroom, with that obscene corpse on its knees before the hamper to keep us company. And here, packed in with us, by God, is Dr. Ernst, the Second Coming of Freud, and Ofelia, the cleaning woman. All of us crowded into a space much too narrow for us, since the Sheridan Square apartment is the old-fashioned kind where the bathrooms were designed for narrow, side-stepping customers.

And no one except me seems to think there is anything weird about it. Or, if anyone does, he is covering up perfectly. It's like that ship's cabin scene in *A Night at the Opera,* the Marx brothers and an ever-increasing company wedged into that closet-sized cabin, each one going about his business irritably but with resignation.

And certainly no one but me seems to take notice of the blood which drips from that body to the tiled floor. A cool company, man.

Ofelia is at the sink. With her usual warped sense of priorities, she is rinsing something in the basin. A piece of notepaper with a message scrawled on it. The scrawl is smudged. Trust her dim Mexican brain to come up with the idea that rinsing it will remove the smudge and leave the lettering. "Will you put that thing down and clean up this floor?" I say to her, but she only darts me a narrow-eyed look of resentment, and, sullen and ponderous, continues working on the notepaper. What is the attraction of this Neanderthal slavey? She comes cheap.

Dr. Ernst leans over to look at the note. "Significant," he says.

"Bound to be," says Irwin Gold. He makes his way around the body on the floor, pushes past me to stand at the toilet bowl. He unzips his fly, pisses loudly into the bowl. Disgusted, I can't turn my eyes from the sight. Unbelievable, the size of that tool. A .45 on a .22 frame.

And the reactions of those around me to this public performance of a private function? Joan and Dr. Ernst, heads together, mutter at each other. Ofelia scrubs her notepaper. The butchered lady in black chiffon oozes blood. Apparently, I am the only one there to even take notice of Irwin's display. "I hope to God you don't put on this kind of show in front of Nick," I tell him.

"Why not?" Irwin finally replaces his pride and glory inside his pants. "He's a fine, big, rugged, well-hung youngster in perfect emotional balance. He's the new breed, Hibben. Able to look at reality with clear eyes. If America is to rediscover its soul, it will be youngsters like that—"

I angrily pull the podium out from under him. "What kind of reality are you talking about, Gold? Don't tell me you also have him stand and watch while you're servicing his mother."

His lips curls. "She now happens to be my wife, Hibben."

"And he's my son. If you think—"

All lawyer, he can't bear to be put down by a non-professional. "Look, Hibben, I'm not here to thrash out your hang-up for Nicholas. I'm here because it's crisis time for you, mister." He jerks his head at the corpse. "Arrest time, trial time, execution time. After which, any and all of your hang-ups become purely academic."

I refuse to let him see the terror this suddenly

churns up in me. "I thought they did away with execution in this state."

"Not for certain crimes." He nods wisely. "Not for certain very special psychopathic-type sex crimes. And from the looks of your victim—"

"*My* victim? What kind of lawyer are you to call her my victim when you don't even know if I've done it? You're out of your mind, Gold."

Now he turns on that Pure Gold sympathy. "Come on, Pete, I'm your friend. I'm on your side."

"Sure you are."

"Pete, you must have seen TV crime shows where a client won't level with his own lawyer, haven't you?"

"What about it?"

"Well, haven't you found that maddening when it happens? Haven't you felt like grabbing the client and telling him that when he's got someone like Perry Mason in his corner, the least he can do is level with him? Those shows may only be pop culture, Pete, but they're full of a wonderful, profound folk wisdom. For your own good, take a lesson from them."

I try to respond to him as one would patiently try to respond to a backward child. "Look, Gold. I never saw that woman before. I didn't kill her. I don't know anything about this whole incredible business."

He points at the gun on the floor. "I suppose you don't know anything about that either."

It strikes me that he is the last person on earth I should have defending me in court. He has too many reasons for wanting to wipe me off the slate. With me gone, Joan won't have me on her mind any longer. She'll be all his, the way she will never be as long as I'm around. Worse, Nick will be all his. The unquestioning, holy faith Nick has in me, the affection he gives me, that will all be Irwin Gold's, once I'm disposed of.

I say, "You suppose right. I don't know anything about that gun either."

"You're lying, Pete."

"I swear to you—"

"Don't perjure yourself, Pete. You know how Nicholas feels about you. It would break that boy's heart if he thought his daddy tried to lie his way out of a tight spot."

The gun is a six-shot Smith & Wesson K-38 Heavy Masterpiece target revolver. It weighs two pounds six ounces fully loaded. Frustrating for Nick after the first round on the range; even a big muscular fifteen-year-old kid doesn't have the wrist for that kind of weight. And it kicked too hard for him. Between the wrist drag and the kick, he was always putting his shots above or below the bull's-eye.

So I had bought him his .22/32 target model S & W, chambered for .22 long rifle bullets and weighing only twenty-five ounces with a full load. What he could do with that popgun on the range was something to see. Wunderlich, the range instructor, said to him last time out, "If we was back in Dodge City in the old days, sonny, I would rather have it out with your papa and his K-38 than you and this BB gun. And that ain't taking nothing away from your papa's shooting."

I picture Nick standing in the doorway of the bathroom, confronting this black-lingeried wench, my gun in his hand. He levels the gun at her, straight-armed, bringing it up to forehead height, lowering it slowly—Wunderlich's style—sighting his target coolly. The front sight is a one-eighth plain Partridge, the rear sight is the S & W micrometer click sight adjustable for windage, which is zero now, and for elevation, which, at this scant distance, is also zero. The woman falls to her knees, holds up her clasped hands, pleads for her life. Nick's finger tightens on the trigger.

There is no shot. Either I can't or I won't imagine the explosion itself, the sight of the gun's recoil, the stench of powder.

But no one else besides Nick and me has a key to

the apartment. No one else could have let the woman in, set her up for the kill. No one else knows where the guns are always hidden away, beneath the clothing in the bottom drawer of my dresser. No one else at all. Only Nick and I.

But he couldn't have anything to do with this horror. I mean, my God, this kid is so straight even his friends put him on about it. Respectfully, of course. He's a little bigger than they are, considerably more mature, a lot more his own man. Most impressive to them, as I've seen out of the corner of my eye, he never loses his cool. Where their voices get louder, his gets softer, forcing them to listen. Where push comes to shove, they know that at boxing, wrestling, karate, you name it, he can take them apart piece by piece, smiling all the while.

And always on the level with me. Always open. Never having to be backed into a corner and third-degreed. How long ago was it he said to me, "You worried about me and the drug culture?"

He knew I wouldn't lie about it. Being open cut both ways with us. I said, "Sometimes. You hear a lot of things. I'd be an unnatural father if I didn't have fleeting thoughts about the problem."

"Well, you don't have to. Not as far as it concerns me."

"Try any of the stuff?"

"Grass. A couple of times. I don't need it."

I had to nerve myself to say it, but it had to be said. "How about the sex culture? Hetero and homo."

His face clouded. "You think because I let my hair grow—"

"You know better than that, Nick. But there's a lot of siren voices clamoring gay is good."

His face unclouded. "Sirens are female, man. Why would they clamor anything like that?"

I had to laugh. "Very funny. But it doesn't answer the question."

"I guess not." He must have sensed the apprehension under that laugh. He said seriously, "I've been thinking about it. Like, if you make it with a guy—suppose he gives you a blow job or something—well, it's no challenge, you know what I mean? It's more like you're being manipulated. But if you make it with a girl, well, you're proving something."

"You are a wise young man, Nick. Matter of fact, you sound remarkably like a wise old man. You come to this through experiment, by any chance?"

"Well, there's this girl— But we didn't ball."

"Just as well. A girl your age is not really as ready to ball as she might make it sound."

"Only this one's a couple of years older than me. Freshman at Hunter. And I think she's ready all right. Except—"

"Yes?"

"Well, like say you're with a girl and everything is set up to ball her. Her folks are away, the lights are low, the whole *shtick*. So when do you ask her if she's on the pill? I mean, you ask too soon, and she thinks that's all you've got on the mind. You ask when you're both in the middle of the hots, and it turns her off. So when?"

Jesus, the romantic problems youth has today certainly are complicated by science.

But Nick talked to me like that. Open. If he had anything to do with these bloody remains on my bathroom floor, he would face up to it. And he is conspicuous by his absence.

Ofelia is finished with her lunatic scrubbing of the sopping piece of notepaper. She opens it, spreads it out, presses it against the tiles of the bathroom wall to dry. It adheres to the wall the way Joan's handkerchiefs used to, back in our multi-bathroomed apartment on East 60th. Walk into Ofelia's favorite bathroom after washday, and there would be a dozen of those almost transparent squares of linen glued around the wall. Everything else went into the dryer, but someone—whoever had smuggled this Mexican warm body across the Rio Grande—must have put the fear of God into her about what to do with ladies' handkerchiefs after washing them. You stuck them against the wall, and eventually they dried, and you neatly folded them without ironing them.

Joan had fits about this the first few times. "No, no, Ofelia. No *necesidad*. Not the wall. What the hell is wall? *La pared*. Not *la pared*. The dryer, same as everything else."

Futile.

I didn't make that mistake. When we divvied up Ofelia after the divorce I got her for one day a week, Joan got her for the rest, and on my day—Friday— Ofelia did what she wanted to the way she wanted to. I let her in at eight-thirty in the morning, saw her hauling out cleaning equipment from the closet, left her to it. When I came home to start the weekend with Nick, he would be there, but never Ofelia. Most of the time, he said, she was ready to take off as soon as he came here from school at three-thirty. Sometimes there was a note left by her on the phone message pad, the spelling a phonetic code of her own devising, the message usually undecipherable. Telling her to please, for the love of God and all the saints in the Mexican heaven, please try to make those messages intelligible, because they are personal, possibly important messages, and I do not permit personal calls to my office by anyone, so I am depending on you, Ofelia, do you understand, depending on you to make those notes readable—telling her this at regular intervals didn't bother her any more than telling her not to dry ladies' handkerchiefs on the bathroom wall.

Now looking at this damp sheet of paper she has just plastered to the wall, I have the feeling she has outdone herself. This one makes no sense at all.

NOSCOOL SONIC COMIC LOC.

Sonic comic. A subtle way of referring to some TV entertainer? *But seriously, folks*— Someone whose mirth-provoking antics on the boob tube could bring a smile even to those dour Toltec features?

NOSCOOL SONIC COMIC LOC

I squint at this mystical message in bafflement, turn to Ofelia. "What the hell does it mean?"

She is silent, her face impassive.

Everyone looks at the note. Dr. Ernst, the Shrink of Shrinks, studies it frowningly. He shrugs. "But how much enlightenment can one expect from such underpaid labor?" he asks the company at large.

I AM IN THE OFFICE of Dr. Joseph Ernst.

I have no memory of the transition, no understanding of how or why it was made, but here I am.

And here is Dr. Ernst at his desk regarding me with a brooding expression, his fat red lips pursed, his brows knit so that the eyebrows make a single dark stroke across his forehead.

The office is changed since my last visit to it no more than a week ago. Vastly enlarged, its ceiling raised. And the doctor used to be an armchair man. Now I am stretched out on an unfamiliar couch facing him. Uncomfortable as hell too, because I am almost, but not quite, on the horizontal, and it takes a painful effort to raise myself a little and look squarely into those contemplative eyes. I realize I am not free to sit up. A broad strap pulled tight across my chest and arms fastens me down to the couch.

Forceable restraint.

I hate physical restraint under any conditions. In my immediate mouth-parching, heart-fluttering state of crisis, it drives me close to panic. I struggle furiously against the strap, but the pain of its cutting into me is too much. I sink back panting.

Am I in the hands of a hired killer? Has this fatuous, jargon-spouting shrink been made Irwin Gold's partner in disposing of me? Gold, who has somehow elected himself my legal counsel, pressing me to take a guilty plea, has not gotten my consent to it. Ernst, for a price, could solve the problem for him. He could

slit my throat and then claim that after confessing to
the murder of the unknown belle, I had committed
suicide right here before him.

Who would dare challenge this? I mean, this is *the*
Dr. Joseph Ernst. Who would doubt him? Not even
my own son, as well as he knows me. And with his father a murderer and suicide—the butcher of a defenseless female and without guts enough to own up to
it—Nick would have every happy memory of me
washed out of him. He would not only be removed
from me but from any kindly thought of me.

Paradoxically, the one hope I can seize on is that
this *is* the Dr. Joseph Ernst. After all, would any man
who spent a lifetime building a reputation like his risk
it all for what Gold could pay him? I don't know.
Fact is, I don't know any more about my analyst than
he knows about me, which, although we've been
dealing with each other for three years, happens to be
very little.

It was at Joan's insistence three years ago that I put
myself in the hairy, grasping hands of Herr Doktor. It
was one of the conditions my wife set to extend our
marriage past what she first decided was its breaking
point. If psychotherapy could repair the short-cir-
cuited wires in our relationship, well, we might still be
able to play house together. So we played house for
one year more until doomsday. Until "I'm getting a
divorce, and you are going to take it and like it" day.

A year of faithful attendance at the confessional on
Park Avenue. A year while I talked and the doctor
made noises in his throat to indicate he heard me.
Sometimes, more or less surreptitiously, he glanced at
his wristwatch. I knew, of course, from the first time
Joan and I sat down before him that he was jealous as
hell of me. Physically, he is a blob, and I am distinctly
not one. Matrimonially, he is saddled with a scrawny
harridan whose father, I had been informed by outside sources, bought his son-in-law's soul by putting
him through medical school. That introductory day,

and those occasional others where Joan appeared at the confessional with me, the good doctor squared his shoulders, sucked in his gut, and glowed with a lustful light. Cooed at my wife, for God's sake, and shook his head in gentle rebuke at me.

Jealous as hell. And when he came half awake in his bed in the dark hours and realized the cold and stringy piece of meat he was rubbing against, why not?

Hope springs eternal. At least I am not yet in the hands of the police trying to explain the bloody horror in my bathroom. Maybe Gold really is on my side. Maybe he is using this means of setting up a defense based on temporary insanity. But who the hell is he to take my guilt for granted?

Dr. Ernst says to me almost affectionately, "Peter, you are addicted to the extraneous. Your thoughts wander, you follow them like a child following a butterfly through tall grass, coming closer and closer to the precipice. This is not good. Now you will please focus on the essentials."

You hear? Ein, zwei, drei—you will focus one time on the essentials. Or else!

And that suddenly acquired Viennese accent of his, which I could swear is phony. It sounds as if he were rehearsed by a retired waiter from a pastry shop on the Prater. Peel away the *alte Wien* from Herr Doktor, and my money says you hit a pure vein of *alte* Brooklyn.

I strain against the strap cutting into my chest. "It's not easy to focus on anything, Doctor, while I'm nailed down this way."

"Possibly. So if instead of a physical effort against that restraint you exercise some intelligence, you will have no more such difficulty."

He's right. I give up the struggle and simply slide my arms from under the strap. I unbuckle the strap. When I move now the feeling that remains suggests that a couple of ribs have been broken by the pressure. I breathe deeply a few times, and the feeling fades a little. But I know I'll have a sweet bruise to show for the experience.

I say, "You were talking about essentials, Doctor."

"Yes. That woman's body. Your gun beside it. Your son."

"My son?"

"Nicholas is a most potent element in this situation. I warned you long ago that your relationship with him is not healthy. You have invested too much of yourself in him."

"And you don't think he's worth it?"

"I think he is an exceptional boy. Any father would be proud to have such a son. But your investment has not been made on that basis. It has been made because he worships you completely, and you have been straining to justify that worship. You have been playing God for him, terrified to let him even suspect your flawed humanity."

The son of a bitch is going poetic on me. But I need him too much to put him down. Need him now, while he stands between the police and me. Will need him later when time for prescription renewals comes. It took hard work to con him into those prescriptions for ups and downs—*Methamphetamine hydrochloric as prescribed, Secobarbital sodium as prescribed*—and I cannot risk cutting off this source of supply. I am not addicted to the stuff, but there are days, two or three at a time, when the curse of the vampire is on me—I come alive in the moonlight, die in the sunlight—and it takes the pendulum swing between chemical ups and downs to keep me going. Since my divorce, those occasional sessions where I bullshit my drowsy shrink for fifty endless minutes at an exquisitely painful rate of pay have only one function: to provide me with the prescriptions.

My flawed humanity, for God's sake. But I take it and like it. I ask, unpoetically but politely, "And what's the prognosis, Doctor? Where do we go from here?"

"Yes. This is the proper attitude. A certain objectivity. So, before we can move in any direction, we must objectively view the condition. Do you have any idea of your condition?"

The Ernst technique. Analyze yourself, then pay a fat fee for the privilege.

I say, "Mentally, I'm confused. Emotionally, I'm badly scared. That tells it all."

"So one must admire your composure."

"I am a full-grown man, Doctor, not a hysterical woman."

"Yes." The Doctor looks me over quizzically. "On the other hand, a state of shock can sometimes be wrongly interpreted as composure. Especially by one who does not comprehend his true condition."

"Me?"

"Of course. At this precise moment, you are in a profoundly dreamlike state due to shock. Your outward composure is an effort to maintain that state and not plunge into coma. Which, I must admit, does not make it any less admirable."

"Thanks." Then I get the full impact of this. "Are you trying to tell me that right now I'm asleep in bed waiting for the alarm clock to go off?"

"I wish I could. Unfortunately, I cannot. That victim of a gunshot in your bathroom is real. That gun—the evidence against you—is real."

"Doctor, I swear to you I did not fire that gun."

"Denial. A familiar syndrome. One commits an act too harrowing to contemplate. A door in the mind slams shut. The memory of the act is locked behind it."

"Killed a woman I never saw before in my life? And right there in a houseful of people?"

"Houseful of people?"

"You were there, Doctor. My ex-wife was there. Her husband. The maid."

He slowly shakes his head. "I was not there. No one was there but you and your victim."

"Jesus Christ, you were all there. I saw you."

More of that inexorable head-shaking. "Why would we be there, Peter? Why would your divorced wife and her husband, both of whom avoid your presence like the plague, suddenly pay you a visit? Why would I be there? Do I make house calls in my profession? And the maid—" He sucks his lips in and out, considering my fat Ofelia.

"Yes?" I feel the comforting warmth of a small triumph. "What about her? She's supposed to be there today. It's Friday. Her day."

"Good Friday. A holiday. More than a holiday for her. A holy day."

"I know. She mentioned it last week. But she said she'd be over anyhow and go to Mass afterwards."

"And did. Do you know what time it is now?"

I glance at my watch and discover I am not wearing a watch. I do some quick calculation. "About one?"

"Exactly one. Your maid arrived at your apartment at eight-thirty. You left her there, and when you returned at noon she was already gone. Is this an accurate reconstruction of events?"

"I don't know. I don't remember coming back to the apartment."

"But obviously you did come back to the apartment. And were angered to find that the faithful Ofelia had worked even less than the half day arranged for. You were even more heated to discover a message she had left on the telephone table—"

"Not on the table. That damn-fool wetback was soaking it under the bathroom faucet. She plastered it to the wall."

"Do you seriously believe that?"

"I make a practice of believing what I see. Why should I believe whatever you want to put in my mind? And come to think of it, what's all this got to do with you anyhow? Who put you in charge of me?"

"*Ach*. Peter, it is at your own insistence that I am, as you say, in charge of you. First in your trauma you turned to your ex-wife's husband. An eminent attorney. A noted manipulator of legalisms. But you got no satisfaction from him. So now it is my turn."

"Then you do know about Gold and me. You did see us together in that bathroom."

"As vividly as you see me now. But only because you have ingested me into your unconscious. You have made me a part of yourself. You are—after three futile years—now for the first time crying out for me, the foolish, windy Dr. Joseph Ernst, to lead you out of the wilderness. To explain to you the seemingly inexplicable. To save you from the consequences of an act which left a corpse on your premises, your gun beside it. Isn't this the truth?"

"The hell it is."

"*Ach,* such perversity. You cry out for enlightenment, and when it is offered you close your eyes to it. But I insist you open those eyes at once. Time is of the essence."

"For doing what?"

"For exploration. For discovery. It is what you should have undertaken under my guidance during these past three years. It is what I hoped you would start to do each time you appeared here."

He exudes an oily solicitude which is infuriating. "I think what you were really hoping for, my friend, was your own chance to explore my wife. Remember her? That sexy little piece who made your mouth water every time you looked at her? For all I know, you finally did get around to humping her right here in this room. And put the visit on my bill. How does that strike you as enlightenment?"

"So. Very significant. The two obsessions come together. The hot jealousy, the cold concern for the dollar. You are in a state of terror, a drowning man, but even as the briny water fills your lungs you clutch to you the leaden weight of these obsessions."

That damn smooth sibilant voice like foam hissing on the beach with the incoming tide. Those writhing lips like creatures living a life of their own under

water. I feel the brine filling my lungs, my breath cut
off. I gasp and choke with suffocation. I manage to
gasp out the conviction that will save me. "This is a
nightmare. A bad dream. That's all it is."

The lips writhe slower. The voice descends to a
basso grumble like a phonograph record coming to a
stop, the needle still on it. "A dream? Then wake up.
All you have to do is wake up."

I cannot.

I can only suffocate in warm, salty Gulf Stream
water. Strong hands lift me above the waves, bear me
back to the shore. My father. "More scared than
hurt," he calls to my mother, who is running toward
us. His tone suggests that my adventure strikes him
funny. Water bubbles from my mouth as he sets me
down. My throat and nose smart from brine.

"Oh, Bubba." My mother kneels down, holds me
tight against her, my chin propped on her sun-warmed
shoulder, my saliva trickling down the whiteness of
her back. "Oh, Bubba, I got such a scare. Don't you
ever, ever do that again."

That lovely Augusta, Georgia, Deep South drawl,
every word rounded and softened. "*Ah got sech a
scayuh.*" Music. And I know the scare is real to bring
her out from under her big beach unbrella. She lives
under that umbrella summer mornings when we make
the trip from Miami to the shore. Never goes into the
water. Never gets her nose pink and peeling. Now, because of me, she kneels there heedless in the sunlight.

"Don't you two make a picture," my father says.

I struggle to release myself from my mother's delicious, sweet-scented grip. "I'm all right, Mamma.
Honest, I'm all right."

I free myself from that grip, back away from it. My
father puts a finger under my chin, tilts my face up,
winks down at me. "That's telling 'em, Bubba. You're
not even scared any more, are you? You'd go right
back in there and swim straight for Europe again,
wouldn't you?"

I squint up at him as he stands there outlined against the morning sunlight. He is huge, powerful, shaggy-chested. The gold filling in an upper tooth shows as he smiles at me. I say, "Yes, sir."

My mother gets to her feet. "Tom Hibben, you want to teach your son how to drown himself, you'll have to do it when I'm not here to see it, thank you."

"Honey, a man gets thrown by a horse, best thing he can do is climb right back on it."

"Well, I don't happen to notice any horses around here, thank you." My mother puts a hand on my shoulder, not hard, just enough to make clear who's in charge. "And I've had enough sunshine and sand flies for today. What we'll do now is go home and have a nice lunch and then pick up Grandma and Sis and go over to the movies. That *Gone With the Wind* just opened over on Flagler Street."

Gone With the Wind. 1939. I am ten years old. It is the first time I am going to see it. Fuck the sunshine and sand flies.

"SPLENDID," Dr. Ernst says. "A superb playback. Every detail recalled most vividly."

He is seated now on top of his desk tailor-fashion, his hands resting on his plump thighs. A weight of disappointment crushes me. I should be starting up in bed, blankets twisted around me from the struggle with my nightmare, bleary eyes straining to make out the illuminated face of the clock on the night table. I should be able to haul myself out of bed and go into my bathroom and find no evidence of murder there. No body, no weapon, no bloodstains. No murder.

But I am not in bed. I am here, with this purse-lipped Brooklyn-Viennese Buddha seated on his desk nodding at me.

"So the exploration begins," he says. "We take the first hesitant step through the labyrinth. The beautiful little mamma shows sharp teeth. And the big strong papa—well, perhaps he was not quite as protective as he could have been. One suspects that he delayed a little before coming to the rescue, *nicht wahr?*"

"Are you saying he wanted me to drown?"

"To drown? *Ach,* no. To suffer a little perhaps. To demonstrate your weakness and his strength. But never to drown. At worst, you were only the mildest of inconveniences to him. More often, he relished his fatherhood. Such a handsome, stalwart little son. So much like his father."

We are on Collins Avenue, my father and I, stand-

ing in the shade of a coconut palm, looking at the
crater where his company is going to build a hotel.
Water fills the bottom of the crater, making a muddy
pond, and men splash around hauling lengths of pipe
and pieces of wood out of it. Pumps, with their lines
in the water, spew it into the street. A man in wet,
mud-smeared clothes comes over to my father. "Have
to pump out the whole goddam lousy ocean," he says.
"Give me up north any time."

"You must like to shovel snow," my father says. He
rests a hand on my head. "My son, Dink."

Dink says to me, "Pleased to meet you, sonny.
Look like your daddy, too. You as tough as he thinks
he is?"

"Just about," my father says.

"Well now," Dink says to me, "how about you
showing me for yourself?"

He gets down on one knee and holds up his fists in
fighting stance. I look up at my father, and he says,
"Go right ahead, Bubba. You know how."

He had showed me how until I had it down pat.
Don't stand off and swing wildly into that out-of-
range face. Move in fast one step, thrust your body
against the out-stretched left arm to immobilize it,
and at the same time jab your own left square into the
face. Jab, don't swing. I move, jab, and my fist bangs
against Dink's mouth. He abruptly sits down on the
sidewalk, looking surprised, then starts to laugh. "Son
of a bitch," he says. He wipes the back of his hand
across his lips and looks at the smear of blood on it.
"A chip off the old block."

"If you want a return match," my father says, "I'm
selling tickets to it."

"So we continue to explore," Dr. Ernst is saying.
"And if all goes well, we must eventually discover reality."

"What reality?" I demand. "What the hell are you
talking about?"

"*Ach.* What reality. The identity of your victim. The reason for your aiming your gun at her. For pulling the trigger."

"Jesus Christ, you keep talking like that, you'll convince me I did it."

"Of course."

"I see. Keep up the pressure until I sign a confession. Once I'm out of the way, my charming ex-wife can slam the book shut. No more ticklish conscience on my account. No more sweating out every weekend when Nick is with me. He'll have to be all hers then. This way she knows damn well he's all mine. She knows he's just doing her a favor living there with her and that prick on wheels she married."

"You accuse me of conspiring with your charming ex-wife to, what you said, put you out of the way?"

I mimic his tone of outrage. "You accuse me of murder?"

"*Ach.* Does a priest accuse a penitent of his sins? Does a surgeon accuse his patient of cancer? This terminology is paranoid. What do I have to do with accusations? Believe me, my business with you is only to separate reality from fantasy."

"Then take a good hard look at the facts, Doctor. I didn't know that woman. I never saw her before. And if I ever was driven to kill somebody, obviously it would not be a total stranger."

"And what was a total stranger doing in your apartment? In such a state of undress?"

"I have no idea."

"I will offer you one. She was there at your invitation."

"Like hell. You said you saw her, Doctor. Did you get a good look at her? Do you want me to describe her in one word? Cunt. Professional, hard-boiled, shopworn cunt. I don't mind paying for my pleasure on occasion, Doctor, but I have my standards. And that specimen on my bathroom floor was distinctly below them."

* * *

I am in the little apartment on Curzon Street. Now and then through the curtained window comes the hissing sound of a car going by on the rain-swept street. It's been sprinkling on and off since I got to London. Tonight it is really coming down hard.

Crystal kneels before the gas heater in the fireplace. There is a pop as she lights it. Her rain-damp dress is drawn taut against the roundness of her buttocks, shows the shadow of the crack between them. I feel a warmth flowing through me even before the heater can take effect.

She gets to her feet. "Whiskey? Tea?" She looks like a wide-eyed, rosy-cheeked schoolgirl. Only the hairdo spoils the effect. It is an elaborate construction, a loaf of golden hair towering perilously high over that schoolgirl face. "Tea," I say. "But first let down your hair."

"Rapunzel, Rapunzel," Crystal says surprisingly. One would not think a girl in her line of work would have this frame of reference. She delicately tucks a stray wisp into the loaf of hair. "Plenty of time for that, luv. We've got all night for letting down things, don't we?" She turns away, reaches for the kettle on the drainboard of the sink, but my voice, like a hand clamped hard on her shoulder, stops her in her tracks. "The hair first."

She shrugs, then sets about carefully undoing her hair. But most of it isn't hers. She lifts if off her head, combs it between her fingers. Her own hair is cut boyishly close. "Disappointed?" she says.

"No." But I am lying in my teeth. I take the wig from her. The hair feels brittle and unpleasant. "What is it? Synthetic?"

"What?"

"Nylon? Something like that?"

"Not bloody likely, luv. Not for what it cost. It's the spray makes it feel like that. The stickum. But it's all real. And all natural blond, same as yours."

"And yours?"

"She hoists up her dress. The panties she wears, what there is of them, have a floral print as if to confirm the schoolgirl image. She draws them down just enough to display pale blond public hair and a very neat, schoolgirlish slit. "And mine," she says.

"Delightful," Dr. Ernst says. "Charmingly presented. But irrelevant and immaterial."

"Not at all. That girl demonstrated what I did buy when I was in a buying mood."

"But tastes change, Peter. They change. They change."

The sun sets on Copenhagen. I enter Tivoli and stroll toward the Koncertsalen in gathering twilight. Suddenly, all the buildings around me in this playland are outlined in varicolored lights. The trees along the path sparkle with tiny blue lights hidden among their leaves.

The girl standing at ease beside the promenade is tall and buxom. She holds an unlit cigarette between her fingers. I stop near her, take my time lighting my cigarette. *"Undskyld,"* she says to me. *"Ma jeg benytte Deres taender?"*

"I'm sorry. I don't understand. I'm American."

"Oh. American." She smiles, gestures at the lighter in my hand, holds up her cigarette. "I asked, please, if I could use your lighter." Her voice is soft, a come-on whisper. Her English is only slightly inflected.

I light her cigarette. She is so tall that her eyes are almost on a level with mine. I glance at her feet and see she is wearing not excessively high heels but sandals. The extreme miniskirt helps give the illusion that most of her height is beautifully curved leg. Her thighs are heavy but solidly rounded, not flabby.

She undergoes my inspection placidly. She parts her lips, lets smoke eddy between her teeth. *"Mange tak.* That is thank you."

"My pleasure."

It is her turn to do the inspecting. Then she says, "You are alone?"

"Yes."

"You would like a companion?"

"It depends."

"I am very talented as a companion. A virtuoso, you know? And discreet."

"I see. And how much does a discreet virtuoso charge for the night?"

"The whole night?"

"Yes."

"For anyone else, eight hundred kroner. But I like you, so for you it will be five hundred. Seventy-five dollars, American."

I shake my head regretfully.

The girl says, "You will not do better, not with someone of quality like me. And do not forget I have expenses. My apartment, any refreshments—"

"We'd use my room at the Regal. And I'd pay for a dinner and any refreshments."

The girl says irritably, "You bargain like a German."

"I'm sorry." I start to move away, but she says, "Wait. For this one time, I will make it four hundred kroner. Sixty dollars."

"Can you figure rate of exchange that fast in German currency, too?"

"Please. I did not mean to offend." She places a hand lightly against my cheek. *"Jeg synes vaeldig godt om Dem.* That is I like you much. I like big men. We will have a good time."

"We might."

"For four hundred. And dinner."

"And dinner. Do you want to have dinner now? You sound hungry."

She gives a small hoot of laughter. "I am always hungry. You know the restaurants here in Tivoli?"

"No. It's my first time here."

"Faergekroen is most fun. Young people, you know? A lot of singing, noise, drinking of beer. But Divan II is best for eating. Very deluxe. And expensive."

"Whichever you prefer."

"Divan II. But it could be at least a hundred kroner. Maybe more."

"As long as you appreciate it."

Her name is Karen, and she is a good eater. After dinner we stroll back to the entrance of the gardens at Vesterbrogade along shadowy promenades and paths. She has given up part of the come-on, the cigarettes, and applies herself with relish to a slender Danish cigar.

"You do not mind?" she had asked when she extracted it from its pack.

"No. Why should I?"

"Most men do, if they are not Danish. And I hate cigarettes. So now I like you even more."

She is surprised by my suite at the Regal. "You said a room, you know, so I thought like any other room. But two rooms like this? Very deluxe."

"My company pays for it. It's supposed to impress the people I'm here to do business with."

"I can understand. It also impresses me much."

Her wry tone suggests she is unhappy at having agreed to perform for a bargain rate in such surroundings.

"But my company does not pay for extras," I remark.

"Like me?"

"Like you."

We shower together, using a great deal of soapsuds and hand-play. Her body is magnificent, firm-breasted and smoothly muscular. She tries to give me a cock-stand, but this white-tiled, sterile room is evidently not the place for it. I give her a finger job, and she puts on a more or less convincing show of ecstasy. There is a faint cigar smell on her breath which I don't find disagreeable at all.

In bed, she takes complete charge, patiently, skill-fully manipulating me with fingers and mouth until at last she raises herself from me, kneels beside me regarding me with concern. "I'm sorry. Might be having the light on makes the trouble. Should I turn it off?"

"No. I like to look at you."

"*Tak*. So if this is all you wish for—"

"No?"

"There is something else? I will be pleased to oblige."

"There might be something else. I'm thinking about it."

She frowns. "It will hurt? That I do not like."

"Can you afford not to like it?"

She sits back on her heels, parts the disheveled hair draped over her face. "Yes. But I have a friend—"

"I'm not interested in your friend. Or in hurting you. My cigarettes are in the other room. Get them for me."

It is heart-quickening to watch her walk, supple, square-shouldered, the tight buttocks flirting with each other. She returns, the pack of cigarettes in her hand, and unlit cigar between her teeth. She lights my cigarette, then motions with the lighter at her cigar. "Is it all right?"

"Yes. And get me a whiskey and water. No ice."

She departs once more, the cigar cocked at a jaunty angle. She brings me the glass of whiskey, sits on the edge of the bed, arranges an ashtray between us.

I ask, "What made you think I'd want to hurt you?"

"Sometimes I am asked."

"But you don't permit it."

"No, I don't. It's, you know, *fare*." She closes her eyes, taps her forehead with a finger, searching for the translation. "Danger."

"Dangerous."

"Yes, dangerous. Anything else, I permit."

"It must be hard for a man to surprise you by now."

"Very hard. You want to try?"

I drink my whiskey, draw on my cigarette, contemplate my playmate. A tension grips my bowels, spreads out steadily. "I might at that," I say.

Dr. Ernst says, "So you cannot dispute me."

"About what?"

"You said you could not possibly have had dealings with that dead woman in your apartment because she is of a type that repels you. And to demonstrate your taste, you offered the delightful little London streetwalker, Crystal. Almost a child yet. Small, slim, barely nubile."

"I don't see—"

"But she was the earlier venture. And soon afterward, given a choice among all the available little Crystals in Copenhagen, you reject each in turn. Now you are inexorably drawn to the Amazonian Karen. A large, cowlike creature whose breath reeks of cigar smoke and who would be quite willing to stretch out naked on your floor and have you drop your shit on her for four hundred kroner."

"Jesus Christ, do you really think I get my kicks from that kind of thing?"

"I only use it as an example of the entertainment your Karen would not hesitate to provide. The point I am making—the point you do not wish me to make—is that she was merely a younger version of that female in your apartment. To use your own words, Peter, professional, hard-boiled, shopworn cunt."

He spaces out the words, coming down on each of them with slow, hard emphasis. They sound extraordinarily ugly, delivered this way.

I say, "I was exercising a harmless whim that night, Doctor. I don't think they've gotten around to executing people for that yet."

"Very clever. But whims, impulses, these things can be most revealing. They often flash a light on strange compulsions hidden in dark corners of the mind."

I feel I am being smothered under a soggy pile of clichés. "All right, Doctor, so now you know that I was driven by a strange compulsion to pick up Karen. And feed her an expensive meal. And take her back to my hotel and screw her."

"Made an effort to screw her, my friend."

"Hell, man, I was pooped to start with. Do you know what the BEA flight from London to Copenhagen is like? The IRT subway in rush hour, five thousand feet up. And I had a week in the London office before that, trying to convince the Old School Tie crowd that you have to spend money to make money in publishing. It would take anybody time to recover from that. I work hard for my money, Doctor. Unlike you, I can't con people into paying me for just sitting and listening to their troubles."

"*Ach,* such evasions." Herr Doktor grimaces. "I tell you, if Virgil had had such a Dante to guide, he would have soon given up the journey as hopeless."

"Then why don't you, Doctor?"

"How can I? Would you let me?"

I am in my bathroom. This time I am all alone with the Belle Époque beauty slumped against my hamper, her head resting on it like a chicken's on a chopping block. My gun is still there on the floor, the strings of blood still marking the side of the hamper, puddling on the floor beside the gun.

For the first time I look searchingly into that pallid face. At the slack mouth, the blood oozing from the corner of it. Strands of dark hair have fallen forward, concealing one eye. I force myself to stare into the other eye, and it stares back at me glassily.

The silence around is so intense that I become acutely aware of the panicky fluttering of my pulse, the whispering of my breath.

"Why not remain in that abattoir?" Dr. Ernst demands. He squats there on top of his desk, the judge sitting on his bench, and I am standing before him, frozen with apprehension. "Why return to me?" His tone is scathing. "For three years I have only been a shrewd little Jew peddling a pseudo-science at exorbitant rates. A quack. A witch doctor. A handy dispenser of dangerous prescriptions. A repulsive lump lusting after the woman you were once married to. Now, suddenly, you give me the great honor of bearing your misfortunes on my narrow shoulders. Why?"

"I don't know. I don't know. But it has to be this way."

"There are others to call on. Priests, ministers, rabbis. Members of the immediate family. Social agencies. In New York City, dial 911 for emergencies. But Dr. Joseph Ernst?"

"Please, Doctor—"

"*Ach,* don't whine, for God's sake. It's nauseating. For my sake, at least, let us have some of that old Peter Hibben *macho.* Some of that famous Peter Hibben cool."

I despise myself for groveling, but still I grovel. "Doctor, forget the way things were between us. They're not like that any more."

"Oh? So now you regret playing games with me these past three years?"

"Yes, for God's sake."

"And you apologize for your deceitfulness? For pretending to accept my therapy? For telling me how successful it was?"

"Yes."

"And you now have complete faith in me?"

"Yes."

"Why, all of a sudden?"

"I told you I don't know. Maybe we've come to understand each other better."

"You flatter yourself," Herr Doktor says contemptuously. "I have understood you from the beginning. No, my friend, the reason for your change of heart is that you have suddenly come face to face with a terrible truth. A murderer must at least know the motive for his crime or there is no peace for him on earth. And in your depths you believe I am the one to unearth the motive for your crime."

My crime?

Jesus Christ, talk about role-playing. A dime's worth of evidence against me, and counselor Irwin Gold turns into Mr. District Attorney. An appeal for help, and Dr. Joseph Ernst comes on like Torquemada.

Speechless, I watch Herr Doktor brace himself on his hands and knees on top of the desk, fat ass waving in my direction. He lies down on his belly, slides backward until his feet hover a few inches off the floor, then with a thump lands on the floor. Disheveled, breathing hard from exertion, he adjusts his necktie, his jacket.

With horror, I realize that he is no more than half my height. A dwarf. The head too large for the body, the body squat and subtly misshapen. I don't remember him like this. Yet I have a queasy dislike for the misshapen human body, the freak, the maimed. Certainly if I had ever seen my analyst in this form previously, I would never have returned to his office again.

He looks up at me, teeth bared, eyes gleaming with triumph. "Mute?" he says. "Tongue-tied? All choked up?" He punctuates each word by jabbing a stubby forefinger painfully hard into my chest. I retreat under the jackhammer impact. I feel the seat of a chair pressing the backs of my legs. The last jab drops me into the chair.

He aims the finger at me. "Admit it. You knew that woman."

"I did not know her."

"As soon as you looked closely at her, you recognized her. And what does this tell us? Your one defense has been that you would not murder a stranger, the woman was a stranger, you would not murder the woman, Q.E.D. But now that you sense she was no stranger—"

"I did not know her."

"*Ach.* Don't you understand you are wasting time with these denials? Do you really think this jury is foolish enough to believe them?"

This jury?

I look across the room. Familiars fill a row of chairs there. A mixed bag of them. Mrs. Gold who had once been Mrs. Hibben. Julius and Jenny Barash, not so much my former mother- and father-in-law as grandparents to my son. Also my immediate kin: my sister, mother, and father, and on the other side of my father a good-looking redhead who, as I watch, slides an arm through his. I fervently hope my mother doesn't take notice of this or there will be a hell of a scene here and now. She doesn't.

And there is my son. Nick. Right on the spot. Frowning at me with bewilderment.

My heart sinks.

"Nick goes," I tell the doctor.

"Impossible. He is essential to the case."

"Like hell. Either he goes or I just clam up."

The doctor glares at me. He motions Gold to him. They hold a muttered colloquy, finally come to a decision. Nick goes. The senior Barashes frantically wave him farewell. When they turn back to me they are still alight with tearful pride. My mother glares at them. On her deathbed, she may acknowledge her half-Jew grandson, but so far she has not. My father, his redhead glued against his side, one of her shapely legs now draped over his thigh, tips me a large wink. If I didn't know him better, I might interpret this as a gesture of sympathy, a sign of our kinship. Knowing him too well, I understand it is only an invitation for me to appreciate his seduction of the redhead.

Thank God, Nick has been removed from the scene. When the time had come where he could appreciate theological subtleties, especially the distinction Stonewall Jackson Presbyterians drew between themselves and Hebrews despite their mutual admiration of Jahweh, the thunder god, I had been honest with my son about the family schism, and he had taken it, age twelve, with his usual good sense. He might be amused now by his big, randy *shegetz* grandpa and his pretty little silver-haired *shiksa* grandma—unlike Grandma Jenny, my mother does not expend effort in camouflaging signs of her age—but more likely he would be cruelly hurt by their rejection of him to his face. Certainly, if introductions were made, my mother would compress her lips and turn away from him. Just as certainly, my father wouldn't do anything to stir up my mother, especially now while he is openly fondling the redhead's torpedo-shaped tit.

Again Herr Doktor and Gold confer sotto voce. Gold approaches me, oozing Rotarian friendliness. "Pete—"

"The name is Hibben, you son of a bitch."

The ooze instantly evaporates. "All right, Hibben, if your one solace is knowing you and Nicholas still bear the same family name, I'll go along with the gag. The point is that we are now about to poll the jury. This can be a painful process for you, but we can speed it up if you change your plea to guilty. Now's the time, Hibben. Once the polling begins, it's too late."

"I'm not pleading guilty to anything, Gold. And what kind of Alice in Wonderland proceedings did this pygmy shrink sell you on, anyhow? First the verdict, then the trial? Crap on that. If you represent me—"

"Hibben, I made a deal with the court. If Nicholas is dismissed from the jury, if he's kept out of the picture, you behave yourself. Work up a scene and you blow it. The boy will be back here filling that empty chair, taking in everything. Is that what you want?"

"No! Under no conditions."

"Then you will behave? You will play it cool no matter what?"

"No matter what? Even being held guilty of a crime I didn't commit? What kind of fancy choice is that?"

"Take it or leave it, Hibben."

I sweat it out, one wave of panic submerging another. "I'll take it. Just keep the boy away from here. And remember"—I nod toward Joan, who sits there wrapped in sweet sanctimony—"if he ever finds out what this is all about, I'll know who gave him the word."

"I'll try to remember that," Gold says scornfully, then says to the doctor, "All right, we're ready."

The doctor points at my mother. "Madam?"

She rises. She removes a postage-stamp-sized handkerchief from her pocketbook and makes a dainty dab at each eye.

"Please, madam."

"Well now," she says, "I was born and raised in lovely old Augusta, Georgia," which comes out *bawn an' rayuzzed,* since the more the invading Yankees and Latins take over Dade County, Florida, the more the sorghum in her speech thickens. "Descended from a long line of highly distinguished preachers and politicians, who each and every one had a direct line to Jesus. Some were even members of the Augusta Country Club. My own dear daddy, rest his soul, once played a round with Bobby Jones himself.

"And there I was, a mere slip of a thing just out of finishing school, almost unbearably beautiful and refined, I assure you, when I was snatched from the family nest by a Florida roughneck who promised me the world on a string. And then left me, time and time again, sitting and holding the string while he went off

tomcatting. I mean, your honor, if it wore a skirt and
stood still, he had his pecker in it before you could
say Deuteronomy.

"Which, after several brief separations from him, I
came to tolerate for the sake of my pathetic, stringy-
haired daughter and my adorable little son, they being
my only solace while their daddy was away hunting
poontang. My little son. What a lambie-pie he was.
An Eagle Scout at fourteen with merit badges from
head to foot. The pride of Miami Glens High School,
winner of six scholastic and athletic awards at gradua-
tion time. A literary light at famous Harvard Univer-
sity. Oh, but the blue blood of my own personal an-
cestors percolated hot in his veins during his innocent
youth.

"But alas, his daddy's blood trickled through those
veins too, and in the end even a mite of pollution will
foul the whole waterworks. In the end, my lambie-pie,
no doubt unhinged by dope and liquor, married one
of Them, settled down among the abominations of
New York City, and denied his own loving family.
True, he phones his aged, but still neat, sweet, and
trim mamma once a week after seven P.M. when long
distance reduced rates are in effect, but only because
of the gilt-edged inheritance he will split with his sister when his mamma and daddy enter the arms of
Jesus, and he doesn't want to do anything that might
risk him his half of the melon. The one virtue still left
in him, praise be, is thrift. That, I am proud to say, I
early brought to flower in him, and the sole satisfaction he might have found in marriage to one of Them
was that They are all born knowing how to squeeze
the last delicious drop of juice out of a dollar.

"Outside of that, your honor, he has no more virtue
left in him than any of that tribe he attached himself
to, what with doing their thing instead of the Lord's,
so that, although I do say it in a voice choked with a
mother's anguish, I still must say yes sir, he is now his
daddy all over again and more than likely to get

mixed up in some wickedness with a female, especially the kind messing up his bathroom floor. Even
unto murder.

"I only pray he will yet take heed to Ephesians
5:5-6 and be saved. Amen."

"Next," Dr. Ernst barks, and at least my father has
the grace to detach himself from his redhead before
he comes to his feet and sounds off.

"Your honor, I tell you I don't know where I went
wrong as a father. I'm just a simple, horny-handed old
real estate dealer, never indulged in any real vice—
despite temptation, I know the Lord wants it to be
done only face to face, with the man on top—and I
was always glad to give Bubba here sound, manly
guidance. To handle a gun, car, and boat so you don't
get yourself killed by them, to fight fair if you can and
dirty when you have to, to respect all decent women
of your own race, including your self-refrigerating
mamma and big-mouth sister, and above all, never to
depend on any cheap rubbers out of a vending machine but buy the best if you don't want a surprise
package laid on your doorstep sooner or later.

"So I did my best, but always pulling against the
current, you might say, because his tight-ass mamma
and sister had their cultured little hooks in him,
hauling the other way. And I lay a lot of the trouble
on Harvard. I mean, what the hell kind of place is
that for an All-State high school lineman? Let's face
it, your honor, an Ivy League jock is just against
nature. But it was his mamma and sister got him slant-
ed toward Harvard and turned from healthy outdoor
sports to printing dirty stories in that college magazine, and after that it was all downhill to perdition. So
it's no surprise he wound up putting a bullet into some
high-price hooker because she was out to blackmail
him or some such. Especially when you figure he was
likely blind drunk on poisonous New York martinis at
the time instead of just feeling good on pure, natural
bourbon."

He sits down and drapes his arm over the redhead's

shoulders, and she crowds close and looks up at him adoringly. "Nobody ever had a better daddy than you," she assures him.

"Which," says my sister, abruptly rising to testify without invitation, "is highly debatable. Speaking, your honor, not merely as sibling to the accused, but also as baby-sitter, body servant, and court attendant to him during his formative years, and speaking with the authority of one who has earned herself an Associate Professorship of the Humanities at Sunshine U. in Miami, Florida, I must state that a father with delusions of satyriasis is not really sound parental material. Nor is a mother who takes out her marital frustrations in incestuous cooings and slobberings over a son who is, at one and the same time, repelled and delighted by them.

"Add to the kid brother's hang-ups, your honor, that he was an incorrigible daydreamer, a dizzy romantic, and sexually precocious. Definitely, although not in the Portnoy championship class, a frequent beater of his meat even before there was any considerable meat to beat. This I witnessed for myself through the keyhole of our adjoining bedrooms, and then, fevered by the spectacle, eventually blackmailed Master Slyboots into mutual masturbation and imaginative by-play. Let me stress, however, there was never penetration. No, indeed. And so faithful have I been to the memory of my peewee Adonis that I have never permitted penetration by any male organ to this day. I admit I do now and then exercise a plastic replica on myself. Reasonably priced, battery-operated, and safely sterile, your honor, it is the instrument which every liberated female—"

"Objection," Irwin Gold snaps, and I am grateful to him for being at least this much on his toes. "Your honor, this testimony is turning into an auto-erotic digression."

With scientific detachment, Herr Doktor surveys my sister's glowing eyes and flushed cheeks. "Sustained."

"Oh, very well," my sister says. "Back to little brother."

"His aberrations," the doctor prompts.

"His aberrations. Yes. Did I mention he was a movie nut? No, I don't think so. And he was. My, oh my, he was. With a special fixation on *Gone With the Wind,* as I recall. Not cowboys, not gangsters, not Laurel and Hardy that season, but *Gone With the Wind,* of all things. I calculated that during its local run he saw it no less than four times, once with the family, three times solo. Charged with this, he frenziedly denied it, his very frenzy belying the denial. He struck back by accusing me of virtually living in the cinema palace showing *The Women.* You may remember that it was directed by George Cukor and featured Rosalind Russell and Paulette Goddard, both at their virulent best. I will not deny that it really turned me on. There was a titillating hair-pulling match—"

"What is this?" Gold demands. "Panty-wetting time again? Objection."

"Sustained," says the doctor. "Madam, it is your brother we are trying to nail, not you."

"Then all you have to do, you wretched little Caliban, is drill deep into his inflamed sense of guilt until he hollers quits. He knows he's a walking pollutant. He corrupted me, he corrupted his wife—God only knows the reason for their divorce—and by constant association he will certainly, sooner or later, corrupt his cherished son. I don't doubt for an instant that he also corrupted that lady now occupying his bathroom floor. And that when she threatened to expose his depravity, he simply put a bullet into her."

I can't restrain myself any longer. "Depravity, hell! Why don't you come right out and tell everybody here the reason you'd like to have me knocked off?"

"Silence!" The doctor scurries across the floor toward me, his face twisted with rage. "Silence! Silence! Silence!" Jab, jab, jab goes that finger into my diaphragm, jolting the wind out of me. "Otherwise

there is no deal. Your son will be back here before
you can wink an eye, taking in every word. He will be
given photographs, recordings, an invitation to examine your victim from head to foot, to examine the
weapon, to judge for himself what happened. Take
care."

"Doctor. Your honor." Here I am, groveling again,
but what the hell choice do I have? "All I want to es-
tablish is that if my sister can get me out of the way,
she inherits my share of the estate. So her testimony—"

"Do you dispute it? Do you say she is lying?"

"Not lying exactly. Exaggerating. Distorting. You
could take any other family—"

"I am not concerned with any other family. I am
concerned only with you. With rendering proper judg-
ment on you."

"Proper judgement? But how can you do that, the
way you're handling this. I'm not trying to get out of
line when I say it, Doctor—your honor—but this isn't
being run like any proper court of law. This is more
like an encounter group, with some poor slob chosen
as victim for the session."

"And where does it differ from any proper court of
law in that respect, my friend?"

"Oh, for God's sake," my sister cuts in impatiently.
My sister does not recognize courts of law or encounter groups. To her, since she took up her profession,
all the world is a classroom filled with nitwits. "The
only question is whether my brother knew that slut.
Of course he did. Just look at his guilty face when I
say it. And either he comes clean right now, or I tell
his laddie boy all about the games his daddy and I
played back in the good old days. In detail."

"You bitch." I want to get at her, but somehow I
don't even have strength enough to drag myself out of
the chair.

My sister smiles poisonously.

"I can read you like a book, Bubba. You knew her.
Now think hard. What was her name again?"

KAREN?

No. Her friend.

The name?

Exotic. Greek. Or sounds Greek.

But it is Karen I am with, my stomach gorged with breakfast rising to my throat as the express elevator of the Hotel Regal plunges to the lobby. Karen, who has eaten twice as much as I did, nibbles on a piece of buttered brioche salvaged from the breakfast tray. As the door opens on the lobby she stuffs the last of the brioche into her mouth, swallows it with a gulp. "Come. I will show you something."

She leads me to the newspaper and magazine shop across the lobby. The woman at the counter is gray-haired, bespectacled, schoolmarmish. She is deep in conversation with a dignified-looking elderly couple. A little girl of about five, their granddaughter probably, is wandering along the long magazine rack which bisects the shop. One small hand has a stranglehold around the neck of a cloth doll. The other slaps each magazine on display as if she is taking inventory. Karen touches the tip of the child's nose with a finger and says, *"Er de papirhandler?* and in answer gets a grave shake of the head.

When we reach the end of the rack where the child has just completed her inventory, I find myself confronted by a display of pornographic magazines, their contents advertised by covers done in glossy sharp-focus color photography. I am relatively shockproof, but still I am jolted by this public display, by the fact that the child has just finished slapping a row of erect cocks and receptive cunts, by the indifference of the elders on the scene, and by the feeling that passers-by in the lobby are staring at me through the glass wall of the shop.

Karen hunts along the shelf until she comes up with the magazine she wants to show me. It is simply and graphically titled *Trio*. She opens it for my benefit, and points. "There," she says. "And there."

There, and there, and on several following pages are photographs of a male and two females engaged in some basic variations of sex play. The shapeliest and hardest-working member of the team is Karen. She studies these representations of herself with interest, her head close to mine. "This was in Stockholm," she says. "The one who made the pictures, Lennart, he saw me here and took me to Stockholm just for the pictures. Two days, and everything paid for."

More than ever I have a sense of being stared at from a distance. I want to shove the magazine back into the rack, want to get away from here, but Karen's obvious pride in this photographic display of her talents keeps me rooted to the spot, inanely making conversation. "Which did you like it better with? Him or the girl?"

"Pete!"

So someone has been staring at me. Vince Kenna, my company's golden boy. Its number one money-maker. Arrived out of nowhere and in one of his manic phases. Red-faced, ebullient, loudly garbed, the caricature of the American tourist. He pumps my hand with that terribly sincere two-handed grip of his. "Pete, baby. I hit London yesterday and Nash told me you were here to sign up Grondahl. Did you meet with him yet?"

"No. Now, Vince—"

"Uh-uh, baby, none of that. I know all about him being Nobel Prize and the last of the giants and the seclusion shit and the rest of it, but it won't kill you to make it a threesome. He might have heard a little bit about me too."

"Vince, he's a sick, cranky old man, not that wild about moving over to McManus & Nash to start with. I'd just as soon—"

"I came all the way from London for this, Pete. Just to get a look at him before he dies. Maybe have a few words with him. Chrisake, he's one of the greatest. He's like Ibsen. You think you can talk me out of a chance to shake hands with somebody like that?"

"You once shook hands with Normie Mailer. Why not settle for that?"

He gives me a look which indicates he does not think this very funny. "Look, buddy, half an hour is all I'm asking. And you don't have to worry about me blowing your deal for you. When are you seeing him?"

"This afternoon. Three o'clock."

"Up in your room?"

"Yes."

"I'll be there. And then grab the evening plane back to London. You going upstairs now?"

"No."

"All right, I can borrow your bed and catch up on some sleep before Grondahl shows."

"You don't have to borrow any bed. I'll get you your own room. You'll be more comfortable that way."

"On the company tab?"

"On the company tab."

Vince looks over Karen, who stands there expressionless. He flicks an eye at the magazines on the rack. He leers at me. "I have a hunch we'd both be more comfortable that way, won't we, old buddy?"

Strøget is block after block of shops, eating places, an occasional movie house. No vehicular traffic is permitted here, so Karen and I are free to walk along the middle of the roadway through crowds thronging it from curb to curb. Karen, who must evidently sustain herself with nourishment every few blocks, is eating her second ice cream cone. But to judge from the crowd around me, it seems to be the Danish way of life, this incessant nibbling at something. A surprising number of children well past infancy tag after their parents, sucking pacifiers.

A bony girl who would instantly be stamped a high-fashion model in New York, her legs like sticks, her face glossy with make-up, her expression the high-fashion catatonic blank, passes by, and the toy poodle serenely trotting beside her not only has gilded toenails, but, more unbelievably, wears sunglasses and has a pacifier clenched in its jaw.

Karen nudges me. "Did you see that?"

"Yes. It looked like something you wind up."

"Not the dog. Her. The way she looked at you."

"No. I was looking at the dog."

"Well, that woman was looking at you. Like she was—you know—" Karen irritably snaps her fingers.

"Thrilled?" I offer.

She gives that familiar little hoot of laughter. "Maybe that too. But I mean with admiring."

"Admiration."

"Admiration. And I like that, you know? Most men are not so big and high as you." She places her hand, palm down, against her chin. "Most men are only this high with me. I am up here, and the man is down there. So people think it is funny. Like would be if I walked now with your friend. The little one in the shop."

"Well, if you run into him again, don't let him know that. He happens to be very touchy on the subject."

"Yes. I could see he is such a one." She frowningly finishes her ice cream before she comes out with the thought disturbing her. "He could make you trouble because of me?"

"You mean because he saw us together?"

"Yes. Men like that, they sometimes make bad jokes about it in front of others. Sometimes in front of a wife."

"No, I don't think he's that much of a fool." An idea takes root in my mind, flowers into full bloom. "In fact, it might be a piece of luck that he walked in on us like that."

"Luck? I do not understand."

"You don't have to. Where are we going?"

"I told you. La Boutique. It's not far now."

La Boutique is a long, narrow shop selling women's clothing, one small room opening into another as in an old-fashioned railroad flat. In the front room, bulky sweaters are on display in glass cases and on wire torsos. A salesgirl approaches us, and Karen says to her, "Fru Gerda?"

The girl points, and Karen leads me back through the rooms, the display of garments as we pass through each doorway changing from ski slope to evening on the town to living room to bedroom. Gerda is in the last room sorting through drawers of lingerie. She is stout, whitehaired, motherly-looking. She greets Karen fondly, gives me a firm handshake. Karen explains our mission, and Gerda says to me, "Your wife's size?" Her English is British-flavored.

I say, "Short and slim. About like that girl you have out there. That salesgirl." I hold my hands out from my chest. "But much bigger here. Large-breasted."

Gerda says with amusement. "Lucky man. About an American ten, I would think. Here, a thirty-six."

Boxes are opened, merchandise displayed. The counter and chairs become littered with negligees, nightgowns, peignoirs, baby dolls. I make my selection. A couple of times, when I am startled by an exorbitant price of an item, Karen, reading my face, says briskly to Gerda, "*For dyrt*. Too much," and Gerda makes no sales pitch, simply puts the item aside. Even so, the bills add up to a prodigal total. Karen takes the final tally from my hand, examines it.

"Rabaten?" she says reproachfully to Gerda, and Gerda, either genuinely unhappy about this, or acting unhappiness with the skill of a master performer, grudgingly pencils in a ten percent discount. It strikes me that this whole thing could be prearranged between her and Karen, a performance calculated to leave the customer content with a victory and Karen in line for a handsome kickback, but I am in a gracious mood and so refrain from voicing the thought.

"And will there be anything else?" Gerda asks me.

"Yes, there will be."

The anything else is for Karen. There is a private dressing room behind the display room, fairly large, furnished with a long, narrow table, an armchair, and an ashtray on a stand, and even more redolent of perfume than the display room. I settle back in the armchair with a cigarette, while Karen, without self-consciousness, kicks off her sandals, peels off her clothing, and models a wide range of Gerda's most exotic merchandise. Just as unselfconsciously, Gerda fetches boxes, drapes their contents on that splendidly naked body, kneels, brow wrinkled, mouth pursed in concentration, to adjust a fold of material, steps back to soberly inquire of me what I think.

I am the decision-maker here, but a decision-maker easily influenced. "Oh, I like this much," Karen says. Or, "This is so beautiful, don't you think?" so that while one small lobe of my brain is doing harrowing arithmetic, the rest of it is cosseted into quick agreement. "Yes, of course. We'll take it."

She is in love with her own body, Karen is, as she poses for me, poses for herself in the huge three-sided mirror that covers half of one wall. Now and then her sense of humor gets the better of her. She narrows her eyes at herself, makes the Marilyn Monroe fish mouth, then giggles at her own pseudo-passionate, hard-breathing reflection. But the humor is only a flimsly cover-up for the very real self-adoration beneath it.

Gerda plays along with this. She murmurs appreciation and turns to me for confirmation of it. Her fingers, after deftly tying a lace or straightening a fold, linger unnecessarily, touching, patting, stroking. It dawns on me that these two females are having a private little orgy here in front of me, and that if there is anything white-haired, motherly Fru Gerda itches for at the moment, it is for me to hie myself off so that she can lock the door and climax the orgy in private.

But it is Gerda who finally leaves, to attend to the packaging of acceptable goods and another adding up of bills. When she is gone and Karen is fitting herself into her body stocking, I say, "You know Gerda pretty well, don't you?"

"Yes. A long time."

"As a lover?"

"No. Of course not. Such a thing to say." But that is the automatic response. Karen shrewdly studies my face, tries to appraise my thoughts. After all, I've already viewed without flinching those photos of her in that magazine, I've already demonstrated a taste for oddball sex, so why not take a chance on seeing what marketing prospects are? She slyly says, "You don't mind when it's two women together? You know. To make love."

"Then you and Gerda have been together like that?"

"No. But she asked. She always asks." Karen makes a face. "But I do not like old and fat women."

"So you always refuse."

"Well"—Karen gives me a confiding wink—"I always tell her some other time. Maybe next week, next month, who knows? So long as she has hopes, she sells me things *billigere*. Less money, you know?"

"Ten percent *rabat?*"

"You say that very well. *Rabat*. But ten percent is nothing. Sometimes when she has very big hopes it is forty or fifty percent."

"That's very clever of you."

"Yes. But you do not mind when it is two women?

You would like that tonight?"

I look at Karen as she stands there clad only in the transparent body stocking. I look at the table piled high with aphrodisiac merchandise. I breathe deep of the perfume saturating the air. "Do you want to know what I'd really like?"

"Yes?"

"Would Gerda object if we kept that door locked for a while?"

Karen walks over to the door and snaps the lock.

"So," says Dr. Ernst. "At the vital moment you cut short the exploration. Why?"

Stunted, gnomelike, he thrusts his face close to mine. His breath is fetid in my nostrils. I try to draw back from it without offending him. As I do so, I see the jury is still here in the office, propped in place like a row of waxworks. All eyes are glassily fixed straight ahead, every mouth is rounded into an O as if preparing to puff out a smoke ring. It is like being confronted by a row of masks representing horror.

"Well?" the doctor demands. "Well? Well?" And again there is that brutal business of jabbing that steely forefinger into my chest to emphasize each repetition of the word.

"I don't know, Doctor."

"Your honor."

"Your honor."

"Also your little tin god, your light in darkness, your hope of salvation, your guide through the unlit caverns of your mind. True?"

"Yes, Doctor. Your honor."

"Because, Peterkin, your punishment is certain. The death sentence has already been pronounced. And since I am only too happy to whittle you down to size, my boy, there is no appeal from this court. None. The one fixed rule here is that he who pulls the trigger pays the penalty."

"But if I didn't pull that trigger—!"

Irwin Gold makes a warning gesture at me. My

helpful counselor-at-law. The Brain. "Hibben, take it easy. Remember the deal. Remember Nicholas."

"Yes, God damn it, I remember." If I must be fried to death to keep Nick from being part of this, all right, you bastards, get the frying pan ready. "But if the verdict is already in, what's the sense of this so-called trial?"

"Look, Hibben," says Gold, but Herr Doktor holds up a hand. "*Ach,* please, Counselor. Let him answer that himself."

"Me?" I look from one to the other of them. "You two make up a set of ass-backward rules and then expect me to explain them to you?" The bitterness of my resentment rises up and sticks in my throat like a sour, half-digested lump of food. "Jesus, this is too much. Why not call off this farce and get right to the execution? Finish it off. *Spurlos versenkt.* Just sit me down in the chair and pull the switch."

The doctor looks interested. "Really? This is all you want? An immediate finish? Execution without enlightenment?"

I don't want it. Suddenly, overwhelmingly, I understand how much I don't want to be blotted out of existence without justification. To be punished for committing a crime makes sense. But to be punished because a crime has been committed and someone must pay for it—

I babble this to the doctor in anguish, pouring out my arguments as if by drowning him in their torrent I can make him feel with me the maddening injustice I'm faced with. He listens gravely, head cocked to the side, a squat, misshapen bird of prey beadily eyeing its intended victim.

"*Natürlich,*" he croaks. "Yes. Of course. An outrage. A gross injustice. Persecution. Kangaroo court. Star Chamber. Constitutional rights. Yes, yes, my friend, scare you badly enough and you become a veritable Demosthenes. But all these simulated pearls of wisdom do not dent the one ironclad fact you are

faced with: you will very soon be put to death for
your crime. Accept that. Give up the implausible ar-
gument against it, that you did not know the victim,
hence—"

"I tell you—"

"—hence you had no motive for firing a bullet into
her. You knew her. You were on the verge of recall-
ing her name. Then you deliberately closed your mind
to it."

"For God's sake, deliberately is the last word I'd
use in my case. Everything that's happened—"

"Silence!"

"Your honor, you're piling injustice on injustice."

"Am I?" The doctor's mouth spreads in a mean,
yellow-toothed smile. "Then perhaps if your son were
given a part in these proceedings—"

"No!"

"You would do anything to prevent that?"

"Yes. Anything I can."

"Ah. Then you will identify your victim, Peterkin.
You were so close to revealing her name when
you walked along Strøget beside your large Copenhagen whore. Think. Remember. A name. A curious
name." Again he thrusts his face close to mine, and
again I flinch from that reeking breath. "What is it?"

Her name.

There is a name. There was a name. "Karen?"

"Nonsense."

"That skinny model? The one with the weird poodle.
But I don't know her name."

"Why should you? Try again."

It is like an insane game of Twenty Questions
where the one clue provided me is the word Strøget.

Strøget.

La Boutique.

"Gerda," I say. "It has to be Gerda."

"You know it isn't."

"No, you're right. Wait." I am hellbent in pursuit
of that name now. Elusive, invisible, it buzzes around

in my mind just out of reach. Not Scandinavian. Greek. Or sounds like it. Bazaar. Bizarre. The buzzing in my ears is deafening now. I reach toward it. I grasp it.

"Papazor! Vivien Papazor!"

And oh yes, oh yes, I knew her well.

VIVIEN PAPAZOR. Karen's friend.

But neither she nor Karen is here in my suite in the Regal. No one is here with me but the steward sent up to arrange a table of smørrebrød and bottled refreshment. I don't know what the hell an ailing seventy-year-old Nobel Prize winner might have a taste for in the way of food and drink, so I have ordered a variety. It looks to me as if there are enough of these open-faced sandwiches and assorted bottles to take care of a regiment. And another worry added to my present surplus. To prepare for the meeting, I've reread all the old man's major novels, the ones that turned me on so hard in my college Lit. courses. Great. Still great. But Anders Grondahl, I can appreciate now as I did not appreciate then, had made a fetish out of the simple life style, had fiercely preached the sweetness of the meager portion as opposed to the bitterness of opulence. By these antique standards, he could be, to use Karen's pet phrase, anti-deluxe. If he now judges from this serving table and these conspicuously opulent surroundings that I am too deluxe for his taste, I am up the creek before negotiations even begin.

Vince Kenna walks in, looks around. He is slightly stoned, probably for courage, and now in a depressive phase. "Didn't he show up? It's quarter after three. You said he'd be here at three."

"He'll be here when he gets here. Take it easy."

Vince looks at the table. "You didn't tell me it would be a party."

"It won't be. It'll be Grondahl and his agent and some guy helps Grondahl get around."

"And me." Vince goes over to the table, points at a bottle thrust into a mound of crushed ice. He says to the steward, "A gin and tonic. And *mucho* gin."

"That is not gin, sir. It is *snaps*. Akvavit."

"It looks like gin."

"Akvavit, sir," the steward says with open contempt. There is no unemployment problem in Denmark.

"Alcohol and caraway," I tell Vince. "Try it. It'll give you the native outlook." This is a man who travels around the world yearning for packaged American white bread all the way. You can take the boy out of the country, as the saying goes, but you can't take the country out of the boy.

He tries a sip of akvavit and does not find it repulsive. He sits down in an armchair with half a glass of it neat and gives me a narrow-eyed look. "What is this with prize winners? First you line up that Prix Goncourt guy in Paris, now it's Grondahl. What's it about? You think the list isn't classy enough with me carrying the ball?"

He has hit the nail on the head. Up to now, the big man on the strictly commercial fiction list of McManus & Nash is Vincent Kenna, a prime example of hack. He writes, in abominable, tin-eared prose, a kind of sexed-up, half-assed *roman à clef,* putting into it the bug-eyed wonder of the country boy observing the city folks through a keyhole. One long, elaborately plotted novel after another, all dealing with thinly veiled newspaper headliners and their supposed behind-the-scenes lives where most of the fun for readers and reviewers lies in guessing who these characters are in real life. Our relationship, Vince's and mine, is based on mutual insecurity. In the process of discovering Vincent Kenna in the slush pile, of showing him how to capitalize on his small talent and turning him into a thundering best seller, I have also built into him the feeling that I am vital to his continuing success. He may not be too much aware of it ninety percent of the time, but that remaining ten percent when morbid doubts of himself paralyze him are enough to keep him from wandering off to someone else's list. And this possession of him—his body may be his own but his soul is mine—bolsters my sometimes shaky position at McManus & Nash. In effect, I am number-three man there, right behind McManus in New York and Nash in London, as long as good old Vince remains their boy. Simple.

So now I say, putting on the indifference, "Don't be paranoid, Vince. You're not really peeved about being on the same list as Anders Grondahl, are you?"

"Nash said he's getting a uniform edition. All twenty books. And high-priced."

"He's never had a uniform edition in English, so it's time he did. Don't worry. Your turn will come."

"That's what you'd like me to believe."

"Vince, a high-priced, fancy, hardcover uniform edition is a memorial. It's a trophy they hand out when the game is over."

"Yeah?" He thinks it over foggily. "Yeah, maybe so. Maybe it is." He gets up, goes to the table, and to the steward's annoyance scours through the neatly arranged smørrebrød looking for something edible like peanut butter and jelly. He finally settles for another belt of akvavit. He takes a sip of it, stands there looking at me with a puzzled expression. "How do you do it?"

"Do what?"

"These snow jobs. I mean, Chrisake, all of a sudden I'm feeling sorry for Grondahl because he's getting a uniform edition. And I know you're selling me a load of crap but I buy it." The alcohol is working on him now. He is taking off from the depressive phase and flying high into the manic. He smiles and shakes his head admiringly. "And not only me. I'm in New York, and McManus says to me, 'Pete's over in London now straightening out that faggot Nash about improving the list. He'll put him in his place,' and then I get to London and Nash says to me, 'Thank God for old Peter. If he didn't know how to handle that bloody McManus, we'd wither on the vine.' Both of them getting a snow job, and both of them loving it. But you know what, Pete?"

"What?"

"Some day they'll get together head to head and find out how old Peter is always snowing both of them, and that'll be the end of him. Right?"

"Wrong. Whatever I say to either of them—"

"—is for their own good. Crap."

"If you say so."

"I say so. And now it's Joanie's turn, isn't it?"

I have been expecting something like this, so I am not taken off guard. I look politely bewildered. "Joanie?"

"You know what I'm talking about, old buddy. I'm talking about your large, economy-size hooker down in the magazine store. The one warming you up with dirty pictures."

"You're kidding, Vince. You really thought that girl was a hooker?"

"Was and is." He is aglow with happy malice. He sits back in the armchair, sights at me over the edge of his glass. "Hit me but don't shit me, old buddy."

"For your information, the lady happens to work for a shopping service."

"Sure she does."

"And if you want to do some shopping for your wife and don't know any more about women's clothes than I do, these people take you to the right places and pick the right stuff. No charge. They get their cut from the seller's end."

He is openly mirthful now. "Sure they do."

"Don't be cynical, Vincent. It's not your thing." I take my time extracting Gerda's sales receipts from my wallet. "Matter of fact, I'm glad you brought this up because I almost forgot about it. I ordered a whole load of stuff for Joanie, but I want to hand it to her myself, so I'm having it delivered to your place in New York, air express. I'll pick it up there as soon as I get back and make a big deal of it when I give it to Joanie."

He says, "Ah, come on," but now he sounds unsure of himself. I hand him the receipts, he laboriously examines one. "For Chrisake, Pete, the way that piece shaped up—"

"Dirty is in the eye of the beholder, Vince. Look, Betsy will be there when the stuff arrives, won't she?"

"Oh, yeah. Sure. I mean, it's school time for the kids so she has to stay in town. But what is all this stuff you bought? How come clothes?"

"For kindling."

"Kindling?"

"Nighties, negligees, undies. Chiffon and lace. Sort of a reminder not to bank those fires too much."

"Oh? Things going that way for you two?"

"Well, my wife doesn't really sit around in curlers and a flannel bathrobe, but she certainly gives the impression of it. I suppose it's just that marriage becomes a habit after thirteen years."

"Yeah, it sure as hell does. But when it comes to somebody like Joanie—I swear, Pete, that woman gets better-looking every year." His face droops into lines of boozy sympathy. "Weird. I mean, for somebody looks as sexy as her."

"I know. That's why I came up with this gag about the nighties and such. Corny but cute. And a lot cheaper than marriage counseling."

"Yeah. Pete, would it be all right if I let Betsy in on this? She'll be wondering about those boxes being delivered there."

"Hell, tell her whatever you want. There's never been any secrets among us, have there? Only tell her not to open the boxes. Not to unpack them. I'll take care of that."

"Yeah, sure." His voice is abstracted. He has a remote look in the eye. He is, poor, jealous little bastard, somewhere far away with my wife, watching her model her porno wardrobe for him, piece by titillating piece.

The scene will turn up in his next book, too. In every book he wrote since he first met my wife, there has been at least one vividly dctailed scene where a petite, dark-eyed, large-breasted, outgoing Jewish girl gets joyously fucked, and I know who she is, and Joan knows, and even faithful old Betsy Kenna knows, which is why she is always pressuring Vince to get rid of the town house and the place on Long Island and migrate to San Francisco, which, she says, is the only civilized place in the United States.

But not for Vince, it isn't.

MY JURY SITS THERE, eyes still fixed straight ahead, faces frozen into that round-mouthed expression of horror. They might be dead, for all I know. Dead and stuffed. There is a temptation to go over and feel for a pulse, hold a mirror before an open mouth to see if the breath of life clouds it.

The doctor, however, seems changed. Still dwarfed, but without that fiery malevolence emanating from him. This could be because he is contending with a problem other than me. He hefts a golf club scaled to his size, a miniature club. He sights along its shaft. On the floor before him is a ball. "Counselor?"

Across the room, Irwin Gold obediently places a drinking glass on its side on the floor, mouth aimed at Herr Doktor. The doctor takes his stance before the ball. He studies the lay of the carpet. He plants the head of the club against the ball. He bends forward, waggles his ass like a cat pretending to spring. He taps the ball, and it travels across the carpet straight into the glass. Plink.

Impatience, like an army of insects, crawls over my skin. "Your honor—"

"Please." His tone is gently admonishing. He plants another ball on the carpet.

Waggle.

Tap.

Plink.

I watch unbelievingly as this stunted Arnold Palmer produces a third ball between his fingers by some sleight-of-hand. The insects swarming over me are devouring me alive now. The protest explodes from me. "God damn it, you're the one who's so uptight about wasting time, aren't you?"

He turns to me. He says mildly, "Did you forget, Peter? It's Good Friday."

"What about it?"

"*Ach.* Friday. Friday. After three years you have no recollection of what this day of the week means to me? It is golf day, Peter. Six days a week, including the whole sunny, tempting weekend, my clientele may pour out its neuroses into my sensitive, always sympathetic ear. But Friday, Peter, it is tranquilizer time for them because it's tee time for me. Now do you remember?"

I do remember. Friday. And Nick coming from school for his weekend with me. Coming at three-thirty to unlock the door of my apartment, to amble into the guest room pulling off his jacket and tie, to make his way inevitably toward the bathroom. The woman's body there, the blood, the gun—

The doctor remarks, "Suddenly you look very ill, my friend."

"I've got to get out of here. I have to get home before Nick shows up."

"Impossible."

"That's what you say." I try to pull myself out of my chair. I can't. I seem magnetized to it. I writhe, struggle, feel the sweat break out on me, drip down my face. The doctor watches my efforts sympathetically. He encourages me. "Good. We try again. Now a little harder. *Ach.* Too bad. Now another try."

I can't even resent it. He sounds as if he really is, quietly, dispassionately, cheering me on. Irwin Gold, on the other hand, seems to relish the spectacle I am making of myself. "You heard him, champ. Another try. One more. What is it with you, Tiger? All talk and no action?"

I make one desperate final effort and feel I am

about to tear apart every muscle in my body. No use. I slump back exhausted.

The doctor says, "You see? Impossible."

"What did you use on me? What kind of drug was it?"

"None, my friend."

"Hypnosis. That's what it is, isn't it?"

"Call it whatever you wish to. The fact is that you cannot leave these proceedings until all the evidence is in. You colorfully described this trial as being run ass-backwards. Very true, Peterkin. Which means it can only be ended when you present the court with a bill of particulars."

"Naming names," Irwin Gold chimes in.

"Explaining motivations," says the doctor.

"That woman's name," Gold says. "Let's have it, Hibben. Jesus, I can't spend my whole life futzing around like this. I've got important things of my own to do."

"Like being buddies with Nick?"

"He'll need a buddy like me when you're gone, Hibben. Better than that, a daddy like me. And don't you think for one second I'm not cut out for the job. Don't you go pulling your football trophies on me, mister. Just ask your son's mamma about who's been giving her full satisfaction in bed seven nights a week, three weeks a month. And with Saturday and Sunday matinees thrown in extra. Admit it. That's the kind of father a boy really needs, isn't it?"

August in Miami is murderously hot, and this is one of the worst days of the summer. And of all times when I should be up to my neck in the ocean I am walking down Flagler Street with my sister, heading for the dentist's office. Hot. Even my sister, who usually looks as if she has just been taken out of refrigeration, looks wilted. Twice she has to stop and polish her eye-glasses, so dimmed are they by her sweat.

But there is no escaping the dentist for us. School

starts in two weeks, and two weeks before the start of every autumn term, Lily and I are shipped to Dr. Murch—that name is a real killer's name—to have cavities plugged and gums investigated by a steel pick that burrows right down to the jawbone and up to the eyeballs. Murder. And since Lily is almost seventeen—more than a year my senior—she is in charge of the party, although I am the one who keeps saying, "Oh, stop squawking. It won't kill you, will it?"

We cross Flagler. We are almost on the other side of the street when a car pulling up to the curb nearly clips me in the tail, and I have to jump to safety. Added to the heat and the thought of Dr. Murch's drill, this is too much. I turn wrathfully toward the car ready to call the driver something that will get me a wallop in the ribs from one of my sister's sharp elbows when I realize there is something familiar about that car. Sure as hell it's the Buick my father traded in a couple of months before in favor of the Packard we now dazzle the neighborhood with. Same blue Buick, no question about it, same Winged Victory brazed on to the radiator cap by our garage man, same wrinkle in the right rear fender which I had made when at dawn one morning I had taken the car around the block without anyone's knowing and come too close to the garage door on the way in. My mother almost had a heart attack when she found out about my being in the driver's seat all alone. My father, I think, secretly admired the feat, although he gave me the back of his hand across my face for it.

"Hey, look—" I start to say to my sister, pointing out the coincidence of the car, when I realize she is already looking. In fact, her mouth is hanging open, her eyes bugging out from behind her glasses like a character in a comic strip depicting exaggerated realization. She says in a gasp, "It's her!"

"Her?"

The driver of the car is getting out of it, locking the door. A girl. A tall redhead, her hair in a snood, her tight skirt outlining the girdle underneath as she bends over to straighten the ankle strap of a shoe. A pretty girl. And young. Very young. And shapely. That round butt aimed at the traffic passing a few inches away from it really gives drivers something to see. A couple of them almost ram each other, straining to see it better. I know how they feel. I seem to have erections more and more frequently and with less and less provocation lately, and here I have a whole pantsful of provocation. I also have the feeling that everybody on Flagler Street is now eyeing my bulge, so I move one leg a little ahead of the other, take a sort of sideways stance that will not make it such a shrieking spectacle.

"Her?" I say. "You know her? Who is she?"

Lily tells me.

"What?" I say blankly.

Lily tells me again.

Now I understand. But my sister's meaningful tone, the pinch-nosed, righteous indignation of her, gives me the angry feeling that I don't want to understand. Lily sees this and is not going to let me off the hook. She is, as my father once told her to her face at the breakfast table, a bitch on wheels. She whispers loudly into my ear, "They do what we used to, stupid. Only she lets him go all the way."

Oh, Jesus Christ, right here on the corner of Flagler and Southeast Second she is talking about what she and I used to do sometimes in my bedroom when the folks were out for the evening and the maid was upstairs in her room with a love story magazine and a quart of beer. I mean, right out here in the open where if a cop hears it I will spend the rest of my life in jail. If I am lucky enough to get put away in jail before my father can catch up to me and beat me to death for my sins. Lily had been the instigator, the experimenter, the blackmailer, but from the time she first laid exploring hands on me I was the one somehow saddled with all the guilt. And, terrified, feel the pangs of it now, the hardening and increasing bulge under my fly making it all the worse.

The girl walks around in front of the car, crosses the sidewalk to the hotel entrance there. Everyone looks at her, especially the soldiers and sailors strolling by. They have been thick on the streets since Pearl Harbor, and I am wise enough to know that from the way they look at any girl in sight, even Lily, they would like to be doing with them what I used to do with my sister. But they are not looking at Lily now. They are looking at the redhead. At her breasts and ass and legs. One of her stocking seams is twisted. It runs from the ankle strap upward in a curving line sideways, up and up to under that skirt where my father—

My father?

And this girl?

Really a girl. She doesn't seem that much older than my sister.

All right, I have finally come to accept the fact that my father and mother—well, that's what happens when you get married. That's why you get married. So you don't have to wait at night until everybody is out of the house except the maid who is upstairs half stewed on love stories and beer. It's all yours for the asking, including the putting-in that Lily denied me. And when you're married it isn't dirty. Well, not so dirty.

But what must go on between my father and this girl is. And why does he fool around with anyone this young? Isn't my mother enough for him? And damn near as pretty as the girl? And—curiously uncomfortable thought—even curvier? In fact, I have taken to backing away from Mamma when she gets one of her lovey-dovey spells. I can't tell her why, which makes complications, but better the complications than the revelation of what happens to my uncontrollable flesh when I am enfolded in those maternal arms. It wasn't like that before Lily had started playing her games with me, but it is like that now. It doesn't even take much more than the mental picture of my mother and father playing those games with each other to build up my pressure to the bursting point.

I watch the redhead disappear into the hotel. Without even intending to, I move a step toward its entrance, and Lily grabs my arm. "Where do you think you're going?"

Where? I am going inside to watch that girl cross the lobby to the elevator. Watch the motion of that rear end and those legs as she walks. I know the one thing about her that matters. She does it. And she is, in effect, family property. So I am going up in the elevator with her, and into her room, and we will do it. All in the flicker of a second comes that wild thought, the heat it sends through my body, and then the sick emptiness of frustration. I say to Lily, "How do you know about her? What makes you so sure?"

"Because everybody knows about her, stupid. Last week she was waiting for him right there in the office. I saw her myself."

"Are you going to tell Mamma?"

"Don't you think Mamma knows? Dirty pig. He's always got somebody disgusting like that stuck away in a hotel room. He picked this one right off a truck farm down near Homestead." Lily's eyes narrow speculatively. "But I'll bet Mamma doesn't know he never did trade in that Buick. He gave it to this one for a present, that's what he did."

Damning evidence. I had wondered why, before the Buick had run up even thirty thousand miles, he had been so quick to trade it in. But giving it as a gift made sense. Dazzling revelation. You give a gift and receive favors. Receive a whole redheaded set of favors.

Dr. Ernst says, "And that was your first view of her?"

"Yes."

"And do you now recall her name?"

"Yes. Vivien Papazor."

"And of course," the doctor says gently, "you felt bitter resentment of the young lady. *Ach.* This Lilith. This insidious alien creature with the alien name burrowing her way into the bosom of your family. Poisoning it. Certainly you felt resentment. Even hatred. Right there at first sight, the seeds of the crime against her were planted. The gun was loaded."

"The hell it was. I never confessed to any crime against her. I still don't."

The doctor chuckles. "True. True. I was using a little trick. Entrapment. A simple-minded device at best. Forgive me."

I am thrown off balance by the admission, stunned by the apology. And Herr Doktor's hitherto flinty eyes are soft now. Luminous with sympathy. How the hell do you figure him? A clever performer? A devious tactician setting a snare within a snare? Not if I'm to judge by that row of jurors. Up to now they have all been wearing those identical masks of round-mouthed horror. Now these frozen figures seem to be taking their cue from the doctor. Every mouth is curved into a tender smile. Every eye is lit with a vacuous, yearning kindliness.

Only Irwin Gold angrily chooses to swim against this sudden and surprising tide of good will. "Tough to crack, aren't you, Hibben? But open up now. Admit it. You hated that girl. She did humiliate your mother. She did drain money out of your father. Even as a kid you had a good idea what it cost to give away cars and pay for hotel rooms. You had to hate her. And that was the beginning of the end for her."

Had to hate her.

The lobby of the hotel on Flagler Street is stifling. A slowly revolving ceiling fan the size of an airplane propeller only stirs up the humid air, does not cool it. The corner where I have been waiting in a straight-backed chair for an hour is the worst place of all; the air here is like a warm, wet sponge pressed into my face. I am almost ready to give up, get out of the place, when I see her enter.

I trail after her into the elevator along with a couple of crop-haired, graying men in officers' pinks. They look her over as we ride upward, give each other covert nods of approval. I follow her out into the corridor, dally while she walks down the corridor, disappears into her room. Then I walk that length of corridor and knock on the door. She calls, "Who is it?" and I say, "Delivery."

She opens the door, and I get my first close look at her. She is very tall. She has pale blue eyes, a snub nose, full lips. Her eyebrows are thinned down to fine dark lines. There is a darkness along the part in the red hair. "What delivery?" she says.

"Car keys." I had stolen the spare set of keys to the Buick long before it was replaced by the Packard and had luckily never gotten rid of them. I hold them up before her. "An extra set for your car."

She takes the keys, looks at them puzzled. "Mr. Hibben send these?"

"No. They're mine." I start to walk into the room, and she braces a hand against my chest. "Whoa, buster. Just who are you anyhow?"

"Pete Hibben. Mr. Hibben's my father."

She is jolted by this. "Your father?"

"Yes."

"He sent you here?"

"No. He doesn't know I'm here. He mustn't know." Suddenly I am in a panic, not understanding how I got myself into this, wondering what can come of it but disaster. My heart is thudding so hard with terror and excitement, I am sure she feels every beat of it in that hand braced against my chest.

I am going to get away from here fast, I am going to take off down the corridor, when the pressure of the hand relaxes. The girl gestures with her head. "Come in here, kid."

I move like a sleepwalker into the room. She closes the door behind her, leans back against it, surveys me from head to foot as if she doesn't know what to make of me. "Yeah, you look like him all right. How old are you?"

"Fifteen."

"Fifteen? You look older than that."

"I know. But it's fifteen."

"Then you sure got a lot of nerve for your age, kid. Now let's have it. What are you here for?" She jingles the car keys in her hand. "And don't shit me it was just to give me these things."

It is the first time any female has addressed me in this kind of language. Even my sister, when we were at our bedtime games, kept her vocabulary primly within bounds. But, dear Jesus, this girl evidently knows no bounds. And she does it. At least, she does it with my father. Goes all the way. And she talks like this. And the way she leans back against the door jingling those keys, her breasts sticking out, and that round little belly, and what is below it, concealed by the tautness of the skirt, and those legs, a little heavy but even more inviting because of that, and oh, dear Jesus, I am ready to black out from all the feelings wildly churning in me.

"Quit stalling," the girl says. "Your mamma sent you here to preach some salvation, didn't she?"

I shake my head.

"No again," the girl says. "Next thing you'll have me figuring you just came here to get yourself laid, if you know what the hell that means."

I know she's expecting me to shake my head in denial once more, I want to shake my head in denial, but I can't. I just stand and look at her like a spaniel with its leash in its mouth.

The gleaming black twin lines of the eyebrows go up. The gleaming raspberry-red lips part. The pale eyes open wide. I hear the pulse banging in my temples while those eyes remain fixed on me unbelievingly. "Well, I'll be goddamned," the girl says.

I say nothing. Speechlessly, hopelessly, I can only stand and watch the fuse I have lit smolder closer and closer to its charge.

"You know you're nuts?" the girl says. "Really crazy in the head or something?"

I must be. I can't dispute this. "I'm sorry."

"I'll bet. Because you know what happens if I tell your father about this?"

"Please don't tell him. I said I'm sorry. I didn't mean anything."

"You meant something all right. But you feel different about it now, don't you? Scared shitless, aren't you?"

She's right, but I can't bring myself to admit it.

"Well?" she says.

Anything to get this over with. I nod yes.

"That's right," she says. "Because you think you're a man, but you're not. You're just a big, stupid, snot-nose kid. Your father is a man, see? Not you. Your father. And I got news for you, kid. You'll never be half the man he is, the best day you'll ever see."

She moves toward a cabinet against the wall, and, the way clear, I start sidling toward the door.

"You stay there!" she says sharply. "I didn't tell you I was done with you yet, did I?"

I stay there and watch her take a bottle of whiskey from the cabinet, a glass from the littered dresser. I am surprised to see her hands are shaking as she pours herself a hefty drink. The mouth of the bottle chinks against the glass, and some of the whiskey splashes on the floor. She takes down her dose in two gulps. She seems lost in thought as she puts bottle and glass down on the dresser. Suddenly she turns to me. "I want to hear you say something."

"Say something?"

"Yeah. And I want to hear you say it good and loud. 'My mother is a dirty rotten bitch.' "

I find my jaws are paralyzed. I can't say it even if I'm willing to. And I'm not willing to.

"Say it! If you don't want your father to find out about this, you better say it!"

Terrifying as the Medusa, she advances on me. Alarmed, I back away. The room is small. Three steps, and I am backed against an armchair in the corner. With a full-armed swing, she slaps my face. "Say it!" Before I can say anything, before I can recover from the shock of that whiplash impact against my cheek, she slaps me again. "Say it!" And again and again yelling that, now hitting at me with both fists while I cower away, afraid to even put a protective arm across my face because that might enrage her past the point of no return, might lead her to carry out her threat to tell my father how I tried to poach on his preserve, might bring final calamity crashing down on me. "Say it! Say it!"

A nightmare. Everybody in the hotel must hear this yelling by now. Or she'll throw a fit right here in front of me, the way she looks and sounds. I hear myself say it. "All right, all right, my mother is a dirty rotten bitch!"

That's the end of it. Her arm, upraised, drops to her side. I realize she is crying, blubbering tearfully. She is a mess. Black tearstains tracking down her cheeks, a wet spot glistening under her nose, the snood holding her hair in a bun hanging loose and the hair down in the back. She can't stop crying.

I take my chances, sidle toward the door making sure I don't even brush against her in passing. I open the door, go through it expecting any instant to be ordered back for more punishment, but she is done with me.

"AT LEAST FOR THE TIME BEING," says Dr. Ernst.

"Trauma," says Irwin Gold reflectively. He is thinking hard. "Trauma. A traumatic experience." He looks inquiringly at the doctor. "How about that for a defense? A dopey kid has a traumatic experience, right?"

"Definitely the experience was traumatic. And scientifically, yes, the boy could be classified as dopey."

"Right. And legally, the child is father to the man."

The doctor raises his eyebrows. "Indeed?"

"Of course, your honor. Or else why the accumulation of data on each and every one of us from the day of our birth? And when a Peter Hibben reaches maturity, do we toss away his dossier and tell him he's off to a fresh start? Not at all. When, middle-aged, he goes berserk, we hark back."

"Your point, Counselor?"

"Simply that it's the child Peter Hibben who's guilty of the crime the adult Peter Hibben is charged with, so it's the child who should be executed for it."

Is this clown serious? I say, "But either way you figure it, Gold, the coffin would have to be the same size, wouldn't it?"

He is serious, by God. He says, "Look, Hibben, when your dossier is turned over to Nicholas it'll show you up as a sexually perverted, psychopathic killer, no matter what. But if we pump some behaviorist bilge into the record—you know, spray Pavlov and

Thorndyke and Skinner all over it—the boy'll get a lot more sympathetic picture of his father. I mean, you take an insecure pubescent kid like this Peter Hibben who's strung out on sex to start with, you throw him up against a volatile agent like this Papazor twat, and what do we have but a lifetime conditioning of the poor kid. After that, all he has to do is hear her name and zap! he goes right for the jugular. It's not his fault. He just can't help himself. So when she unexpectedly shows up in front of him again years later—"

"Unexpectedly?" Dr. Ernst says. "In her underwear?"

"Why not? Maybe he made her peel down before he put that bullet into her. Made her show herself for what she was. The ultimate humiliation."

The doctor turns toward the jury. It shows no reaction, offers no sign of life. "You see?" the doctor says to Gold. "A waste of breath. Behaviorism rings no bells here."

Gold shrugs. "You can't say I'm not trying."

"For a double-cross," I say. "You miserable bastard, you told me Nick wouldn't have any part in this if I went along with your cockamamie trial. But you'll make sure he gets all the dirt sooner or later, won't you?"

Gold's lip curls. "The only deal I made, Hibben, is that if you play ball, Nicholas is kept away from these proceedings. Or do you want him standing here right now, looking at you that way he has?"

I am chaining the bikes to the railing in Central Park, and Nick is standing there, looking at me that way he has. A little reproving, a little amused. Despite my mood, it gives me the tickling, pleasant feeling that he is the older of the team. I say, "All right, my friend, then I am overcautious. But better that than having a couple of black cowboys rustle them in front of my eyes."

"I wish you didn't talk like that."

"I wish I didn't have to."

"Uh-huh. Another kindly conservative."

"Oh, oh. You sure know how to hurt a guy, don't you?"

We smile at each other, understand each other. There are things we don't see eye to eye on, and the trick is never to become humorless about them. We climb halfway up a hill and sit down, backs against a rock. We sit in silence. I pluck a stem of grass, work its tip down one side of my jaw, up the other.

"Well?" Nick says.

"I don't quite know how to put it. I'm trying to think of the best way."

"Usually the shortest way, no?"

"Yes."

"Well?"

"Well, it's final now. You and your mother will be moving in with Grandma and Grandpa tomorrow. Day after, she's going down to Mexico to get the divorce papers."

"Alone?"

"Yes."

"Don't you think I should go along with her."

"No. She doesn't want anybody along with her."

"But isn't it kind of a rough place? I mean—"

"I know what you mean. But the Mexican lawyer and his wife are friends of Mr. Gold. He's already been in touch with them about it, and they'll keep an eye on her. Meanwhile, you keep an eye on Grandma and Grandpa. It'll be a bad time for them too."

"Uh-huh. And they'll be thinking the same thing about me." He shakes his head regretfully. "I wish I didn't have to be around them while they were getting used to it."

"It can't be helped. What the hell, Nick, it's a bad time for all of us."

We sit in silence again. Finally he says, "What did happen? What went wrong?"

"I don't know. Things. A lot of things."

"Me, for instance?"

"No. Absolutely not you. Jesus, don't you ever get that idea in your head."

"I can't help it."

"You'd better help it. Take my word for it, when it came to the wind-up you were the only good thing we had together."

"Then what did go wrong?"

"I told you. Things. They change. Look, two people start off together and it's fine. It works fine. But people change. That's the only sure thing in the world. People change. And that can mean that whatever they had between them at the start gets lost along the way."

He gives me that look. "Grandma and Grandpa didn't change."

I think it over. I consider Julius and Jenny Barash when I was first led into their apartment by their daughter. I say to my son, "Sometimes I wish you weren't half Jewish. That's the half that makes you such a hairsplitter."

"A *pilpul*."

"Is that the Jewish word for it?"

"Hebrew word. But Grandma and Grandpa didn't change, did they?"

"They did. But I suppose the differences between them never went as deep as the ones your mother and I have."

More silence. I watch the foot traffic on the walk below and try to think of some magic words that will instantly heal all my son's wounds. But there are none. I couldn't make myself eat breakfast; now I am nauseated by hunger and bleak depression. I want to cry, but that is unthinkable.

Nick says, "When will I see you?"

"Every weekend, if you like. I'll be getting a place further downtown—around the Village, I guess—and it'll have a room for you. All yours. You can come right from school every Friday and stay over until Sunday evening."

"Do Grandpa and Grandma know that?"

"It's all part of the agreement. They know it."

"Well, all right. I mean they're always worrying about everything, so I'd hate to—"

"No, they'll understand when you're not around on weekends. And you won't be staying with them very long anyhow. You and your mother'll have a place of your own as soon as Mr. Gold finds something suitable."

I am learning that the best way to handle it is by talking off the top of my mind this way. A brisk, businesslike stringing together of clichés. Meanwhile, keep the eyes front, don't look at Nick, just focus on the blacks and Puerto Ricans dribbling popcorn, candy wrappers, beer cans all over the roadway below. I pay them welfare money—extortion money—so they can buy that crap, and then I pay the Sanitation Department to pick up after them. In return, they jumped my son on his way from school, sent him home with a knife slash in the arm, blood soaking through his shirt sleeve.

I can't help myself. I look at him now and find he is looking at me, and, Jesus Christ, I should have let Joan be the one to give him the word the way she wanted to, but I didn't trust her to do it fairly, didn't know what she'd say or how she'd say it, so here I am on a Sunday morning in Central Park driving the nails into my only begotten son, and what has he ever done to deserve it but trust me?

THE DOCTOR STANDING THERE, regarding me somberly. The waxworks jury. A dream. A nightmare. Of course, a nightmare.

Break the spell, for God's sake. Now.

I clamp my teeth into my lower lip and bite down hard. It hurts. I am not imagining that hurt. I bear down harder, desperately willing away the pain, but it only increases. Almost fainting from it, I feel a warm trickle down my chin. Blood?

The doctor says to me, " 'Why the children? Why must the children be hurt?' Do you know who wrote those words, Peterkin?"

"Dostoevsky. In *Karamazov*."

"You are an admirer of his? Have been since you discovered him during your college years?"

"Yes."

"And of Tolstoi, Turgenev, Flaubert, Joyce, and Mann? Certainly of Papa Hemingway."

"Yes."

"So. Because, Peterkin, that is the dream. Not this trial, but the dream where you, the new Maxwell Perkins, discover the new Dostoevsky, the new Hemingway, and raise them to glory. Find them as acorns and raise them to be oaks in the literary forest. And in the end there will be a splendid volume titled *Letters to Peter Hibben,* tributes to you from all these young giants, which will be Required Reading. Too bad."

"Why?"

"Because the end is so near. The dream, Peterkin,

must always remain a dream."

Gold says tartly, "As far as I'm concerned, your honor, the end isn't near enough. If we could only—"

"Of course, Counselor." Herr Doktor motions at the jury. "Next."

For a few seconds there is no response. Then my son's grandparents rise from their seats together. The mouse and his mate.

"Barash," the grandfather says. "Julius Barash. And wife, Jenny. Your honor, I'll put it in a nutshell. I don't want any part of this."

"Pop, be reasonable," Gold says. "You know he was capable of killing that woman. All you have to do is say so."

"All I'll say is he gave me a wonderful grandson."

"That has nothing to do with it."

"Then I'll also say he's been a sick man for a long time. Very disturbed, you know what I mean? And between you and me, Irwin, I'd rather pity him than give him a kick in the pants."

He pities *me,* for Christ's sake. This all-time loser who has spent his life being bullied by his wife and daughter, swindled by everyone he does business with, robbed regularly at gunpoint by enterprising *shvartzehs* to whom he meekly hands over his hard-earned money without even whispering a protest—this is now what is pitying me.

I can tell from Gold's expression that he finds this at least as grotesque as I do. But shrewd as the weasel who discovers he can't corner the mouse, he abruptly changes tactics. "All right, Pop, let's leave murder out of it. But what about the reason Joan divorced him? You remember the reason, don't you?"

"I don't want to talk about that either."

But why not, I wonder. What the hell is so sinful about two people discovering they're incompatible? He should rejoice in that incompatibility. It gave him more proprietorship of Nick than he ever dreamed he'd have.

Gold is openly sore. "Ah look, Pop—"

"Let him be!" Jenny says. She clutches her husband's hand. "This is a saint on earth, this one. An angel. What are you picking on him?"

Gold is instantly placating. "I'm not picking on him, Mom. But the vote should be unanimous, and he's just being stubborn about it."

"Because he can't stand to say bad about even a degenerate. So I'll vote for the both of us." She points at me. "Take my word for it, Judge," she says to the doctor, "he's a monster. A sexual pervert. Killing some poor helpless woman would mean nothing to him."

I look at Julius. If ever there was a time for this mouse to let out a squeak of protest, it was now. But there is no squeak. Being bullied, put down, spoken for was his way of life. He was not going to convert from mouse to lion now for my benefit. And Nick getting cues about how to be a proper man from this sad sack!

I say to the doctor, "Is this your idea of testimony? Getting witnesses to charge me with any damn crime that comes into their heads. Murder isn't enough, so now we're into sexual perversion? Peter Hibben stands exposed as Jack the Ripper? Jesus, this has to be a nightmare."

"It does?" The doctor squints at my face. "I thought you had already put that theory to a very painful test."

I move my tongue across the cut on my lip, feeling the sting of it, the warm salt wetness of blood. "If it isn't a nightmare, Professor, you don't know what a fair trial is all about. If you want to get at the truth—"

"Knock it off, Jack." He is suddenly changed again. Gone is the precise diction with its Viennese flavor. Now the speech is pure waterfront Brooklyn, grating out of the corner of his mouth. He sounds mean and he looks mean. In fact, he bears an uncanny resemblance to Charlie McManus, my tough-guy publisher boss, who intrigues the more genteel inhabitants of the literary world by looking and sounding like a gangster in an old movie. All the doctor needs to fill the role of dwarf gangster is the snap-brim fedora and cigar butt. He says, "Because I don't buy crap. And you got a name for being a real crap artist, Jack. But the music has stopped, baby. The waltz is over."

The change in him has me off balance. "Your honor—?"

"That's who I am."

"Your honor, all I'm getting at is that you're the one who talked about my unconscious, about guiding me through the unlit caverns of my mind, that whole—"

"Sure. And I'm doing my best, Jack. Except I never figured it would be like traveling from New York to Yonkers by way of Hong Kong. That's some mind you got there."

"Isn't that how the unconscious works?"

"Maybe yes, maybe no. But you showed there's plenty of conscious working there too, the way you damn near chewed your lip off. Look at it. It still hurts bad, don't it?" Unthinkingly, I run my tongue over it, and he can tell from my reaction that it still hurts bad. "See? So your only job is to get shaped up before your time runs out. Line up the facts and look 'em over. Or you'll never know what the hell you're here for."

"But facts—"

"Facts. Like that dame leaking blood all over your toilet. You gonna tell me she's not real?"

"No."

"You mean you know a fact when it comes up and hits you right in the face?"

"Yes."

"Like, it's a fact today is Friday?"

"Yes."

"And a little while ago, around noon, you ducked out of your office and went home? You figured to wait there until your kid shows up from school?"

"Yes."

"And when you got home, that Mexican zombie who sweeps up around the place wasn't there?"

"No."

"But somebody else was?"

"Somebody else?"

"You know who I mean, Killer. That Vivien Papazor piece. Right there in your bed waiting for the action to commence."

"I swear to you—"

"You swear too easy, Killer. She was there. All juicy and ready. And you know what happened then? You couldn't get it up, and she needled you about it. So you shot her."

"She wasn't there. I don't remember anything like that."

"Then what are you sweating about? Look at you. You look like you just took a bath with your clothes on."

I feel the cold sweat drenching me, feel the tooth-chattering chill of it penetrate my whole body. "She wasn't there! She couldn't have been! I don't remember anything about it!"

THE HUSKY YOUNG MALE NURSE helps Grondahl on with his coat as gingerly as if the old man were made of glass. The agent says to me, "Call downstairs, will you, Peter? Tell them Herr Anders Grondahl is ready to leave and wishes an elevator to be waiting."

I hesitate only a moment, then pick up the phone and relay this message to the desk, braced for God knows what kind of nasty comeback. But the clerk only says, "Of course. An elevator for Herr Grondahl," in a tone which suggests we are arranging for the safe transport of a national treasure. Which, come to think of it, is not so far from the case.

Vince Kenna is high as a kite, head bumping the clouds. He says delightedly, "Herr Anders Grondahl's personal elevator. Now that's what I call service, Maestro," and the old man laughs that wheezing, emphysemic laugh of his in appreciation of the compliment. His English has proved better than competent, and he and Vince have gotten along swimmingly from the start. There is nothing like the brashness of a Vincent Kenna to fortify one in the presence of the great. And nothing like the awe-smitten regard of a Peter Hibben for an Olympian to make him feel like an extra on the scene, functioning best only when it came to offering a pen for the signing of a contract. And Vince, the son of a bitch, had removed the keepsake pen from the Olympian's hand after the signing and tucked it into his own pocket.

The contract. There it is on the desk, and Vince or no Vince, it is the contract I have made a reality despite every obstacle. "Wait a minute," I say, and take the contract into the bedroom, lock it safely away in my attaché case, plant the case on top of the dresser as one would a trophy.

I realize the woman keeping herself company in the room is smiling at me. I smile back. Vivien? Vivien. Karen's friend, acquaintance, proxy? Time enough to clear that up later. But definitely she has Karen's good sense when it comes to these things, because she has not made herself one of the party but has stayed out of sight in the bedroom from the start. She smiles at me now, winks broadly, and I feel a tickle of anticipation in my crotch. One party is over, another, it seems, is soon to begin, and this time without Vince Kenna to pollute it.

I am high now myself when I rejoin my guests in the living room, and, in fact, we are all high as we leave the suite, loaded to the Plimsoll mark with food and alcohol and good will. Sure enough, there is an empty elevator parked at the end of the corridor, its operator barring the way to an indignant couple who want to get aboard.

Vince and I are following a few steps behind Grondahl and his aides when Vince pulls me to a standstill and says in an undertone, "Anders is dropping me off at the airport." *Anders,* for Christ's sake. One of Vince's buddies, like Ted Dostoevsky.

"That's nice of Anders," I say.

"Damn nice. It's not even on his way home. Look, Pete, you want to do me a favor?"

"Any time," I lie.

"And it's a favor for the company too. As soon as we're gone, call up the airline and see if they can't have a PR man and a photographer waiting for us at the terminal building. Right outside there. It shouldn't take more than a couple of minutes to get some pictures of Anders and me together. Will you set that up? Maybe somebody from a news service would be even better. How about it?"

I should have known.

"It's short notice, Vince, but I can try." Not that I will.

When we all reach the elevator, the couple being refused admission into the car is having it out with the operator. They are plump, middle-aged, and tweedy British. "But see here," the squire is whinnying at the operator, and the operator responds with boredom just short of an open yawn, "I said already, you must wait for the next."

Then he waves these would-be intruders aside, and, as if mesmerized, they move aside so that Grondahl and party can step aboard, Vince close on their heels. Grondahl unleashes a thundering fart. He gives me a wicked smile, pats his belly. "Maybe you have done me a little too well, my friend. *Mange tak,*" and as the elevator starts to close, I am inspired by akvavit and foresight to bow deeply to the old man. The door closes tight.

The Britishers are looking bewilderedly at me. The man says, "Now what the devil—" and I press a finger to my lips, cutting him off in mid-question. "Please. His Majesty would be very angry."

"His Majesty?" The man gapes at the elevator door. "That was the king? Of Denmark?"

"Incognito. So please, you have seen nothing. You will say nothing."

"No, no. Of course not. Quite understandable." They look ready to remove their hats and hold them to their hearts. "Oh, quite."

"*Tak.*" I give them a curt bow. I wheel and walk down the corridor, hands clasped behind my back for their benefit, head obviously filled with affairs of state.

Vivien.

But first to clear the mental and emotional decks. In the living room, I phone for room service to clear away the table. Then I do some serious wall-to-wall pacing. Counting in my Prix de Goncourt boy, I have now nailed down a couple of high-prestige and low-earning international prize winners to the McManus &

Nash list. This will give my bosses a chance to savor glory when the news is made public. Later, however, red ink may flow. Trouble in the offing. Big trouble for a not very big publishing house whose credit at the bank is already overextended. And how do I prepare for it? My nerves—every strand from neck to knees—wind up tight as I consider unlikely solutions to the problem.

The hell with it. Anders Grondahl's contract is there in the bedroom. Lay your hand on it and feel the magic.

And Vivien is there in the bedroom too.

THE RADIATOR BEHIND ITS LOUVER busily clicks and hisses, yet the bedroom is uncomfortably cool. I realize a chill nighttime breeze is stirring the window curtains. I shut the window, stand looking out at the flatness of Copenhagen, gray against black. Far below is a subway station, its dimly lit platform exposed. A toy train pulls into the station, toy passengers spill out of the cars. A large sign on a building down the block blinks on and off, casting a green haze every time it blinks on. BOWLING.

Vivien lingeringly runs a hand up and down my naked belly. She says, "What a town. No wonder Hans Christian Andersen had to cook up a dreamland for himself."

"There's always Tivoli Gardens."

"Dreamland with sausages and slot machines. Close the drapes too."

"No one can see us here. We're too high up."

"I know. Close them anyhow."

I find the cord, draw the brocaded drapes together.

"They're dusty," Vivien says. "The way you're being overcharged here, the management ought to be told about this."

"The company's paying the bill."

"In that case, don't bother."

Unclothed, she kneels before the open dresser drawer, examines the assortment of Fru Gerda's merchandise Karen had stored there. She tests chiffon and lace between her fingertips. "Very deluxe." Her accent is not a bad imitation of Karen's. "Kind of a classy slut, that Karen. In her own fashion."

She stands, poses before the closet mirror holding a nightgown against her. She is as tall as Karen, but heavier. And where Karen uses cosmetics sparingly, this one's lips and nipples are brightly reddened. The differences go deeper. Karen is cool and plays it hot. A shrewd pro, she knows how to turn up the gas when you talk money. Vivien is not playing hot, she is hot. Surveying herself in that glass with half-closed eyes, her clenched teeth showing, her nostrils flaring, she is not adoring her own body as Karen does at such moments, but is contemplating the purpose it is obviously intended for. It is a functional unit, this body, and it is the function she adores, not the body.

She slips on the nightgown over her head. The reddened nipples show darkly through the smoky gray material. "How do you like it?" she asks my reflection.

"I like it."

She studies the view with heavy-lidded concentration. She raises her arms ballet-dancer style, rests them on her head. "No objection to the hairy armpits, I trust."

"No. But it's a little unusual, isn't it? I mean, for an American female."

"Oh, I've been international for a long time, darling. And more than a little unusual." She turns away from the mirror, looks meaningfully first at me, then at the bed, and I say, "No rush."

"I see. The anticipation is half the thrill. Like going to the dentist."

I laugh. She looks inquiring, and I say, "Now I know who you are. The first time I ever saw you, I was on my way to a dentist."

"That day in my hotel? The delivery boy with the car-key bit?"

"No, the day before. On Flagler Street. You were getting out of your car. The first view I had was all ass and legs. You bent over to fix your shoe right there in the middle of traffic."

"Wedgies with ankle straps. I used to do that deliberately. Stir 'em up on old Flagler Street."

"You sure as hell stirred me up."

"I know. And how about a drink to sweet memories?"

"Akvavit and ice?"

"Will do very nice. If Mr. Grondahl's ice hasn't all melted."

Despite my call to room service, no one had showed up to clear away the mess on the refreshment table, and from what I knew of the Regal's service by now, I was sure no one would until the chambermaid made an appearance in the morning.

Vivien looks distastefully over the remnants on the table. She picks a sliver of chicken from a slice of soggy bread and nibbles at it. "Mr. Grondahl and entourage would seem to be hearty trenchermen."

"They are."

"A Danish vice."

"Among others."

She says, "I like the others better. Any ice left in that bucket?"

A handful of ice chips float in the bucket. I drop them into a glass, pour akvavit over them, give the glass to Vivien. She says, "None for you?"

"I'll take turns with you."

We take turns until the glass is empty, and then she says, "But it paid off, didn't it? Mr. Grondahl is now your property."

"He is."

"You know he'll probably lose money for your company, don't you?"

"He might."

"And that French genius you just signed up. He's not likely to break any sales records in America either, is he? Or England?"

"Not too likely."

"And those hairy unknowns back home you've

lately taken under your company's wing in return for their great unwritten masterpieces. Risky investments, aren't they?"

"Highly risky."

"And all that just to get the taste of Vince Kenna out of your mouth?"

"That might be part of it."

"What's the other part? Plain, old-fashioned hero worship?"

"Nothing wrong with that, I trust."

"No. But it does make kind of a curious pantheon, doesn't it? Big Daddy Tom Hibben back to back with Anders Grondahl."

"Look, dear, suppose you let me worry about the little paradoxes in my life."

She shakes her head. "Except it's long past worry time. From the look of those little bottles in that night table, it is now nerve-twanging time. Capsule time."

"More like lecture time, the way you sound. Come to think of it, you do know a hell of a lot about me, don't you?"

"Everything that matters, darling."

"While I don't know much more about you than your name."

Her laugh is uncannily like Karen's little hoot of amusement. "And Vivien isn't really my name."

"What is?"

"Never you mind. That part of me is gone and for-gotten."

"How'd you happen to hit on Vivien?"

"Oh, that. Remember *Gone With the Wind?*"

"Vivien Leigh?"

"Yes, indeed. My elected godmother, you might say. I was mad about her. Total identification."

"You poor kid. Abandoned by Clark Gable before you even had the braces off your teeth."

"Not while I was Scarlett. I knew damn well when he walked out on her at the end, it wasn't really good-bye. He'd be back bright and early and horny next morning and give it to her right there in the hall.

Right there on the floor."

"Too bad they left that out of the picture."

"My feelings exactly. But the fact is, darling, it's better that you don't ask questions about me." She thumps the empty glass down on the table. "Is that hall door double-locked?"

"Don't change the subject, Vivien."

"Sorry, darling, but I just happen to be a very private person. A little psycho about it, in fact."

I snap home the bolt on the door. We go back into the bedroom, a tension between us. Vivien settles into the armchair. With elaborate disregard for me, she draws up her legs, plants her feet wide apart on the seat of the chair. The hem of the nightgown, at first stretched taut by her knees, slithers down and settles in folds above her crotch, concealing nothing.

"Another way of changing the subject?" I say.

"Darling, this is the subject." Slowly she spreads her knees apart until they're pressed against the arms of the chair. She watches me, smiling a little at the mounting evidence of my reaction to the display. "You see?"

Without warning, I backhand her across the face. She looks stunned, then as I raise my hand again she shields her face with her arms. "Don't! Please!"

"Sorry, dear, but even at discount rates I owe you at least a couple of dozen like that. Remember back in Miami when you were Daddy's girl friend how you put Sonny in his place? How you belted him around, knowing he wouldn't do anything about it?"

"Pete, that was so many years ago!"

"But unforgettable. You can see what an impression it made on me."

"Pete, darling. Please—"

She cowers away, looking so terrified that I lower my menacing arm. And those widespread knees look so inviting that I have to fight down the urge to step between them and vent myself in her at once. I roughly push her feet to the floor, drag down the nightgown to conceal temptation. "Lady, you're the one who invited herself here as Karen's replacement. You're the one pushing the hard sell. Which kind of shapes this up as a buyer's market, doesn't it?"

"My God, Pete, I'm not here to sell you anything. I love you."

"Love me? I'm afraid you're confusing me with my father, lady. Didn't you once tell me at the top of your voice I'd never be half the man he was?"

"Yes, but I—"

"And have me hand you back your opinion of my mother as a dirty rotten bitch? Recite it to you loud and clear?"

"Yes, God damn it!" Now her temper is overriding her fear. "And I was also the little girl your daddy was keeping. A teen-age kid from the boondocks, already hitting the bottle. The one he kept promising to marry as soon as he could get a divorce."

"And you believed him?"

"I wanted to. Until you walked in on me that day."

"And?"

"And that was the end of it between him and me. For good. I knew you were what I wanted, not him."

"Well now, Scarlett. Too bad you didn't let me know about it when it happened."

"No." She shakes her head furiously. "I didn't want you to have me the way I was. Poontang. An easy lay from the other side of the tracks. There had to be more to it than that. But I knew there couldn't be, the way I was. So I had to change. I had to make myself over into someone different. Someone you could love."

"Now that's what I call a noble ambition." I press my fist to my heart. "You know, it kind of grabs me right here."

She says with desperation, "Pete, don't talk like that." She gets to her feet, moves close against me, and I see her eyes are glimmering with tears. "You wanted the truth about me, didn't you? Now that you have it, is it really too hard to take?"

"So," Dr. Ernst says. He regards me tenderly. He is again the pseudo-Viennese dwarf, not the snarling pseudo-gangster dwarf. "A touching scene. Deeply touching."

"I don't see it, your honor," Irwin Gold protests. "If you ask me, that dame was at least as much of a weirdo as my client."

"Of course. Crazy, one might say, as a bedbug. Yet she plucked these ancient heartstrings, Counselor. Consider that early in her life, this pathetic child, this bird in a gilded cage—"

"Your honor, it happened to be a back room in a third-rate Miami hotel. And she was a boozy little bitch taking a horny real estate operator for all she could get. Including a Buick with less than thirty thousand miles on it."

"But she was soon to be redeemed by her love for a good man."

"What man? For Christ's sake, this was a fifteen-year-old boy. A high school kid with his head full of football signals, and a permanent hard-on."

"But tall and strong far beyond his years, Counselor. A fit prince for this Cinderella. An inspiration for her. And once their paths crossed, she was inspired by him. Destined for the gutter, she rose high above it. I found it very affecting."

"Maybe I would too, your honor, if it turned out this piece died in bed of whooping cough or crud or whatever killed that broad in *Love Story*. And if she was wearing a flannel nightie and was clutching a Bible when she breathed her last. But considering that she was knocked off by a thirty-eight slug in the defendant's bathroom and was dressed for the occasion like the star attraction at a stag party, I can't share your sentiments."

"I am not the one on trial here, Counselor."

Gold wheels around to face me. "How about it, Hibben? This Flagler Street chippie boots you out of her way so hard you bounce when you hit the ground. Thirty years later she miraculously turns up at your hotel in Copenhagen right out of nowhere. A woman of the world. Sophisticated. Wealthy. Mink-lined, middle-aged pussy. And it seems that the only thing she had on her mind all those years was a picture of you and her holding hands as you walk into the sunset. Come on, Hibben. What goes here?"

What goes here? Birth pangs. An incipient ulcer coming to glorious, agonizing flower right in the spot an insurance doctor had tapped with a condescending finger. *Duodenal,* he had said. *Tensions work on it like sandpaper.* And oh, how right he had been. The sandpaper is working on the raw meat now. Thrust, pull. Thrust, pull. The pain in waves, excruciating on the thrust, only a little diminished on the pull.

That's what goes here, Counselor. Now are you happy?

"Hey, mister," Vivien says.

I open my eyes. The window drapes do not quite meet; a pale, watery Danish sunlight shows between them. Vivien is standing beside the bed looking down at me. Her nightgown is on the floor along with my blanket. She says, "All right if I use your toothbrush?"

"Christ. After last night you even bother to ask?"

"Just being polite. You know something? You look real beat up. All passion spent."

"Not quite."

"Glad to hear it, stud. We've got a long day ahead of us."

"I'm afraid not. I'm here on business, and the business is finished."

"Grondahl's business. Not mine."

"I'm already booked for the noon flight to New York."

"Then you can just unbook. You know I'm the therapy you've needed for a long time, darling. And we've hardly started the treatments."

"I'm sorry, Viv. No dice."

"Conscience?"

"Call it conscience."

"You mean you really were infected by all that churchgoing and psalm-singing your darling mamma used to lay on you? And giving you those great big wet-mouth kisses for collecting Sunday School cards? But you're a big boy now, Bubba."

"That's the rumor."

"So you can't still believe God has nothing better to do than keep tabs on your quaint little sins, can you?"

"Hardly."

"Oh dear. I wish you could say that with more conviction."

The trouble is that she's getting through to me. Not only because of the way she stands there naked—a hefty earth-mother hopefully waiting to be raped—but also because we seem tuned in to the same emotional wave length. I relish even the way she puts me down. Quick and sharp, the lightweight words a concealment for heavyweight feelings.

I sit up, swing my feet to the floor. "Viv, all joking aside—"

"All joking aside, darling, I think I rate at least as much of your devotion as Karen did. Or Rapunzel."

"Rapunzel?"

"Mmm. A mere fortnight ago. That London lovely with the hideaway on Curzon Street. The kiddie with all the store-bought hair."

"Crystal. How the hell do you know about her?"

"Proximity. New York, Paris, London—whither thou wert, I wert. I'm surprised you sometimes didn't feel me breathing down your neck."

"You've been that close to me that long?"

"Sometimes so close, mister, that if you suddenly turned around, you'd be looking square into my melting eyes."

"Then why did you wait until now to make your move?"

"Because it had to be made at the right place and the right time. When you were far, far away from your adorable, man-eating little wife. And when you finally understood that she was a lot more man-eating than adorable."

"But those two days I was with Crystal—"

"No, that meant you still weren't ready. She was too much like the girl you married. The small, sassy, cutesie kind. Oh, you were shopping around, all right, but you were shopping the same old merchandise. Not so good for me. But when you found that Karen sent out the right vibrations, it was very good for me."

"Hell, I'm beginning to think you planted Karen right there in Tivoli as bait."

"Nope, she just happened to be there. And if she weren't, you would have picked up somebody just like her around the next bend. Because you were finally ready for the type, man. My type. No more pushy little Joanies who keep making demands on their men, but great big easygoing females who only want to know what makes the master happy so they can get to work on it."

"The answer to Women's Lib."

"That's your Vivien. I like brassieres and lace panties. I dote on those sheer nighties and see-through goodies packed away in that dresser. And I'll make you a fair offer. You phone the airline and postpone your flight, and I'll start the day with a real harem show. You'll be the sultan and I'll be the harem, and

I'll model every one of those anti-Lib garments for you until we find out which one turns you on the most. And along the way, whenever your blood pressure starts to get out of control, I'll provide instant relief. How does that strike you?"

"You know damn well how it strikes me. But let's be practical, Viv. I've got an office in New York to worry about. Another in London. A neurotic word-machine like Vince Kenna to keep oiled up and producing. Not to mention a wife and son who expect me to join them for dinner this evening in New York."

"There's an old Chinese saying I just made up, mister. One honest reason is worth more than a thousand hollow excuses."

"I'll have breakfast sent up now, Viv. After breakfast, it's good-bye."

"Sure. Don't look around, just let me remember you this way. What's the honest reason, Pete?"

"Viv, it's been great up to now. Don't spoil it."

"It gets better as it goes along, darling. And I'm not the one spoiling it."

I go into the bathroom, step under the shower, turn on the cold water full force. Vivien watches from a little distance. She flinches as cold spray mists her body. She backs away, starts to laugh helplessly. "The Boy Scout treatment, for God's sake! Oh, poor, terrified darling."

THE PHONE ON THE DESK is ringing but no one picks it up. I can't. The doctor and Gold seem deaf to it. The jury remains in its coma.

Just as well. Nick was here at the start, he could be calling to ask me what it's all about, and I have no intention of telling him. Now or ever.

The ringing stops. Good. But a grim picture I once before visualized is again planted in my mind. Nick, standing in the doorway of the bathroom, leveling that gun at Vivien Papazor. Nick, confronting his family's nemesis, blindly revenging himself on her. No one else has a key to the apartment. No one else knows where the guns are hidden. If I wasn't the one who pulled the trigger—

I realize Gold is speaking to me. "I asked if you're ready for questioning, Hibben."

"You can skip the questions, Gold. I want to confess to the murder. I killed her. That's all there is to it."

"Ah, come on, Hibben. Quit playing games."

"Look, I'm admitting my guilt. Isn't that what you want?"

"The hell it is. You know you've already been found guilty. The question is why you killed her."

"Because she bothered me."

"Oh? But you didn't shoot any other women who bothered you that way, did you? Like your wife, for instance, before she dumped you? Or any of those asswigglers around your office who seem to think you're the greatest thing to come along since pantyhose?"

"No."

"Which makes Vivien kind of a special case, doesn't it?"

"Yes."

"Very good. Two nice straightforward answers in a row. Now let's see how you do on this one. Why was she a special case, Hibben?"

"You saw her in action, Gold. She wasn't looking for any one-night stand. She wanted a lot more than that. A lot more than I was ready to give."

"Love, sweet love?"

"Call it that if you want to."

"Well, if I don't want to, Hibben, you can just blame it on those home movies you've been unspooling."

I hold my hands wide in appeal to the doctor. "Your honor, if my attorney refuses to believe my testimony—"

"Your honor," Gold says angrily, "if my client thinks his hokey scenarios prove anything—"

"Wait. Wait." Herr Doktor motions both of us into silence. He scrambles up into his chair, plants his elbows on the desk, props his head in his hands. Finally he addresses Gold. "Of course you understand, Counselor, that what you call home movies are, in fact, projections of the defendant's memories, offered in good faith and without intent to deceive."

"Granted, your honor. But he has a memory like a four-handkerchief movie. Pure meringue. From these last samples, I say that in the clutch he sees exactly what he wants to see."

The doctor considers this. He nods. "Yes, the theory has merit. Certainly his condition when Vivien entered the scene invites serious consideration of it. Excessive tensions heightened by alcohol and amphetamines. And then all is released in an explosion of sexual activity. The episode could be traumatic. It could result in memories which are largely wish fulfillment. Yes. As you say, Counselor, it adds up to a large portion of meringue on a very thin crust of reality."

"Coming from such an eminent psychotherapist, your honor," says Gold, the canny shit-kicker, "your approval really grabs me. It also leads me to suggest that in some previous scenes my client showed us—"

"No, no, Counselor. You have my assurance that all previous scenes were presented accurately. Untampered with. The conditions creating trauma only existed when Vivien was present. This was the crisis time for him, this scene. It marked the very first exercise of a fatal wish fulfillment."

"So this is it?" Vivien watches me lay out my luggage on the bed and start to fold jackets and slacks into it. "Absolutely no more postponements?"

"Absolutely."

"But at least you don't have to take the noon flight. There's another at six. It would give us most of the afternoon."

"You want to get me lynched? You heard me on the phone with my wife yesterday."

"I heard you. And I didn't like what I heard, Pete. No man your size should cringe that way."

"Exercising diplomacy, dear, is not cringing."

"You were cringing. You sounded guilty as hell. Like some kid trying to lie to his mamma about those sticky spots on his bedsheet."

"Let's not get nasty about it, Viv."

"Don't you mean serious about it? Because really, what's the sense of just one of us being serious about all this?"

"That's a good question."

"Then how about a good answer?"

I don't answer. The closet emptied, I turn to clearing out the dresser. Vivien says, "Can you deny that these were two of the best days you ever had in your life? The most fulfilling?"

"Come on, Viv. I've had good days before this."

"With a woman? Any woman?"

"I don't keep score. I don't have a little red book full of pluses and minuses."

"Shifty, aren't you? Quick on your feet for such a big fellow."

"But low in spirit. Viv, do you honestly believe I want to sign off like this?"

"Yes."

"You know better than that."

"I know too much. I know that right now you're like somebody with a royal hangover. Sick, dizzy, ashamed, and full of noble resolve. Never again, says you. It was fantastic while it lasted, but, hell, this kind of thing can become a habit."

"You said no tears, no fuss. Why not stick to it?"

"Because one of us has to have guts enough to be honest. And don't think I believe that low-in-spirit shit for a second. You're programmed to enjoy the repentance just as much as the sinning. You know they go together. It wouldn't be half as much fun for you if they didn't. Low in spirit? Man, you're tingling all over right now with a wonderful, electrifying sense of guilt."

"Right. And any time I stop tingling with guilt, you'll be glad to recharge me."

She makes a sound which is half convulsive laugh, half snort of outrage. "I hate you, you smart-ass son of a bitch."

"No you don't."

"No I don't. I love you, you sadistic son of a bitch. Rotten, perverted Boy Scout. I dare you say out loud that you love me."

"I do."

"Do what?"

"Love you. And these two days really have been fantastic."

"Every Boy Scout's wet dream?"

"No, a lot more than that."

"How much more? Be serious. Really make me know it."

"All right. I put it all together when I'm with you. I become the quintessential me. Wide open and receptive. Savoring whatever comes my way. One gigantic, probing, responding nerve."

"I do declare. I sound like an acid high."

"And that is why I'm now signing off, sweetheart. Too much acid and you can wind up permanently walking upside down on the ceiling."

"How do you know you're not doing that right now? Which means that another dose of me would just turn you right side up."

"I know it. And you know it. And our two days are over. And, for the record, I don't anticipate any more like them for us."

"Oh, but I do."

"Viv, be reasonable."

"I am reasonable. I'm not the one behaving as if what we've found together is something terrifying I have to run and hide from. And what you call signing off, I call turning off. That's what throws me. The way you turn off so easily. Turn on easily, turn off easily. Like a goddam electric appliance with an automatic timer in it."

"A job and a family make a highly effective timer, believe me."

"Am I trying to take you away from them? You know I'm not."

True. I do know it.

Having played the right card, she instantly follows with another of the same suit. "All I want, Pete, is an understanding between us. I'll never knock at your door unless I know you're alone behind it. But when I do knock, you're to let me in."

"Sweetheart, that door happens to be in New York, four thousand miles away."

"Wherever." She watches me open the bottom drawer of the dresser which is stuffed with lingerie. "What a pretty pile of goodies. But you can't walk into your apartment with them. Not with everything there your exact size. And with those interesting stains and lipstick smears. It would be a complete giveaway."

"To say the least."

"So just leave all this with Gerda on your way to the airport. She can ship it to some safe address in New York along with those things you bought for your wife."

"They're going to Vince Kenna's address."

"Oh? You mean you had all this planned in advance? That's why you did all that expensive shopping for your wife?"

"Clever woman."

She puts on an expression of wide-eyed wonderment. "Me? Why, Rhett Butler, you old flatterer."

IRWIN GOLD IS JUBILANT. "Did you follow that scene closely, your honor? That lingerie bit? That's what I call pay dirt. Absolute evidence that Mr. Muscles here is transvestite. A cross-dresser."

"True, Counselor."

"True?" I can hardly get words out, the pain of that flaming ulcer is so intense. I have the feeling this pair of inquisitioners are taking turns grinding an abrasive into it. "You call an insane accusation like that true?"

"Peterkin, Peterkin, a diagnosis is not an accusation. And that alluring lingerie which you just displayed to us was your size."

"So was Vivien. So was Karen. And they were the ones you saw wearing it."

"Also true. But remember that you are now projecting memories for us which are unconsciously reshaped to suit your image of yourself."

"And what you want is an image of me flouncing around in ladies' undies."

"You find that so horrible to contemplate? A harmless aberration which undoubtedly dates back to the dawn of mankind? To the prehistoric era when clothing first took on sexual significance?"

"I find it sickening to contemplate. And I don't think my lawyer knows what evidence is."

Gold bristles. "Look, Hibben, you picked up Karen because a big girl like that made cross-dressing easy for someone your size. You bought the stuff, the first time in your life you ever did that kind of shopping.

You kept it when Karen took off. You shipped it home. If you don't think that's solid evidence, I'd like to know what you've got up your sleeve to disprove it."

"Not up my sleeve, Gold. Right there at the end of that row of waxworks."

Gold looks. "My wife?"

"My ex-wife. Get the truth about me out of her, and you'll have what I call solid evidence about the kind of man I am."

"Your honor," Gold says, "I don't see why my wife—"

"The truth, Counselor. Above all, the truth." The doctor tenderly regards Joan, who sits with hands clasped demurely in her lap. "My dear child."

She gracefully rises to her feet, once winner of the Evander Childs High School Award for Best Posture and still champ. "Your honor?"

"You won't mind describing the intimate details of your relationship with the defendant?"

"No."

"Which began—?"

"Very soon after McManus & Nash hired me as his editorial assistant. I really had it bad. When I was called into his office, it was so bad that my stomach would turn over and my hands shake."

"He was that attractive?"

"Well, your honor, he was a big, handsome, ballsy jock among a collection of very wispy males. He had good schooling and good manners. And it was obvious that as long as he was willing to take the crap Charlie McManus dished out, he had a glowing future with the company. All in all, the perfect love object for any virgin editorial assistant whose brain, during this phase, resembled nothing so much as a large, soggy matzoh ball."

"*Ach*. How easy for him to take advantage of this."

"In all fairness, your honor, I must admit that I was the aggressor from start to finish."

"He resisted?"

"Ineffectually. After all, I was not without my charms. Not quite as *zoftik* as I am today, but still an authentic little beauty. Almost as important, he had no allies to encourage resistance to me. No family within range. No trusted friends."

"None at all?"

"Not one. A casual acquaintance with a few men in the office and at his athletic club, that was it."

"A bad sign."

"Not from my point of view. I wanted no competition from any direction. I wanted total possession. When his family informed him they would not show up for the wedding, I enraged my mother by expressing satisfaction at this."

"Then you never met his family?"

"Never. However, each Christmastime for a number of years I made a point of sending them a Chanukah card. Eventually, the defendant caught me in the act. He was furious. He was always ambivalent about my Jewishness, rather enjoying it among our circle, but making it plain that I was not to rub it in his family's face."

"So. But on early acquaintance you had no real clues to impending trouble?"

"Well, let's say I deliberately closed my eyes to some real clues."

"Such as?"

"For one thing, he was tight about money. I didn't know then that those who are tight with their cash tend to be uptight about their emotional coin as well. They seem to regard the generous and open giving of love as a form of overtipping."

"And besides this danger sign?"

"Besides this, there was from the very first time we went to bed a peculiar aspect to our sex life. I mean, looking back at it, damn peculiar. I should have admitted that to myself the very first time with the defendant when he tried to make the earth move."

"He did not succeed?"

"Nothing moved. In the end, we settled for our first honest outgoing conversation where he confided to me that never before in his life had he gone to bed with, so to speak, a civilian. He had been laid for the first time at the age of sixteen, when, along with some members of his high school football team, he had shared in the gang-bang of a buxom high school roundheels who then penalized them each a dollar for her services. A week later, enraged when none of the bangers would pay her further attention, she had them all hauled in for rape. The case was thrown out as soon as it was learned that she had taken money from them. What seemed to loom largest in the defendant's mind was that while his mother went into a hysterical fury at hearing about the affair, his father was extremely proud that he had finally had his cherry copped. Patted him on the head for it, and rewarded him with an expensive hunting rifle the defendant had long coveted."

"Symbolic."

"Almost as symbolic as the name his father had given him. Anyhow, from that time on, the defendant had bedded quite a few females, but always professionals. Faced at last with pristine, vacuum-packed, amateur pussy, he just couldn't cope."

"A classic problem."

"With a classic solution. The next time out, I was all the whore he could ask for. My nightwear, my manner of authority, the works. Hell, I did everything but ask for my money and check him for clap before he took his pants off."

"You were not repelled by this role?"

"On the contrary, I found myself both entertained and excited by it. So was the defendant."

"Then the experiment was a success?"

"It was."

"And afterward?"

"The same. For many years."

"You also shared a meaningful relationship?"

"Well, we talked. We exchanged opinions. We didn't

agree on a lot of things, but still we communicated. And he was a devoted, patient, adoring father to our son. He was always at his best with Nick. Most fathers in our circle seem to regard their children as irritants. Not the defendant. In fact, he took charge of the larger part of Nick's bringing up."

"There were no conflicts between you over this?"

"Sometimes. But nothing serious. It was just the way that the jock in him surfaced when it came to Nick. He kept pushing masculinity for the sake of masculinity. You know. The mighty hunter, mighty warrior *shtick*. But whatever conflicts we had—"

"Yes?"

"Well, they could always be resolved in bed. Without words. And no holds barred."

"During those years. But then came a change?"

"It did. A cooling-off process set in. The defendant performed listlessly in bed when called on, and then, to escape the need to perform at all, he pleaded fatigue, tension, all those textbook excuses which make just enough sense to be convincing. When the excuses started to sound hollow, he adopted that cruelest of devices: the deliberate contriving of arguments and the retiring into hurt silence where all lines of communication are cut off."

"And your conclusion?"

"The obvious one. Simply that he was shoving it into some other woman. Still, I wasn't sure. But three years ago, soon after he returned from a business trip to Europe, I had all doubts erased."

"You obtained proof of his infidelity?"

"I obtained proof of his guilty conscience: a large luxurious gift of intimate garments bought in Denmark during the trip."

"But a gift, dear child—"

"Up to then his homecoming gifts to me were, unfailingly, token bottles of perfume. Now to suddenly present me with this expensive, carefully selected assortment of silks and laces could mean only one thing. Furthermore—"

I RING THE DOORBELL and brace my shoulders, prepared to face zero temperature again. Joan was chilly before I made that Paris-London-Copenhagen swing, she was chilly when I returned from it, but it was, infuriatingly, my extravagant homecoming gift to her—cost plus duty, $780—which seems to have brought her temperature down to zero. Without saying it in so many words, she made it plain that this was the bouquet the erring husband buys the little woman on his way home from the whorehouse. It makes a nice climate to come home to after the office grind, a sample of outdoor life in the Antarctic.

Furthermore, Ofelia doesn't open the door for me, and I have to wrathfully dig out my keys and let myself in.

Inside the apartment, Ofelia is not sluggishly making her way to the door.

Nick, my apprentice bartender, is not at the sideboard in the dining room where he always stations himself on my arrival ready to swirl the stirring rod around in the pitcher of martinis.

Joan is nowhere in sight.

The apartment seems as mysteriously abandoned as the *Marie Celeste*.

It isn't. Joan stands there in the middle of our bedroom surrounded by wild disorder. The drawers of my dresser are wide open; one drawer lies upside down on the floor. The suitcase in which I had smuggled Karen's lingerie from Vince Kenna's place is open on the bed, its locks wrenched loose. The bag's contents are scattered around the bed and floor.

One glance is all I need, and I think, God almighty, if there's a divorce I lose Nick. There he goes, there goes everything that means anything to me, and I'll have to spend the rest of my life hiding behind lampposts trying to get a look at him as he goes by across the street.

Joan says hoarsely, "Close that door," and although I can now guess that Nick has been hastily shipped off to his grandparents, Ofelia given the night off, I automatically close the door behind me.

Joan presses her hands to her cheeks. "Oh God, this is awful. I thought I could cope with anything. I can't cope with this. Do you understand, Pete? I don't know what to say. I don't know what to do."

"About what?" Above all, I must stall for time. Improvise. Ride with the punches until I can somehow counterpunch. I have no ready answers for her. I had locked the stuff away in that valise, hidden the only key, planted the valise under another on the top shelf of my walk-in closet. Incredible that it should have been dragged out into the light by anyone else, forced open, the contents examined piece by obscene piece. "Joan, what the hell is going on here?"

"Pete, listen to me——"

"If what you wanted was an explanation of that stuff——"

"Pete, please, please, listen to me. I know the explanation. Crazy as it sounds, I'm even grateful I finally understand what's been happening between us these last few months. Now all I want you to do is be honest with yourself about it. My God, transvestitism isn't any crime, it's a sickness. So all you have to do is admit you're not well. That you need professional help. Pete, there's this Dr. Ernst I heard speak at the New School——"

"Does he deal with cases of compulsive suspicion?"

"What?"

"Wives who snoop through their husbands' closets

hunting for evidence against them. You can't cope? Jesus Christ, how am I suppose to cope with that?"

"No," she says between her teeth, "you are not going to turn it around that way. Make me somehow feel guilty the way you've been doing. And that's another thing. Something really rotten. Telling Vince what went on in our bed."

"I never did."

"You told him, and he told Betsy. I wondered what got into that bitch all of a sudden. Talking to me about premature menopause. About seeing a gynecologist who could handle my kind of problem. About how once a month when she's dutifully willing to let Vince climb on her she puts special pink pillowcases on the pillows to let him know it. Suddenly being so damn kind to me. So sympathetic about my problem. Until I finally asked her yesterday what the hell problem she's driveling about, and she gets highly insulted. After all, she says, if you can confide our sexual problems to Vince, I should be able to confide them to her. Then I knew. You were covering up your trouble by blaming it on me. But to people like that? My God, Pete, that fucking, self-righteous ecological disaster with her six stupid brats was actually triumphant because she could finally put me in her class. Make me out to be the same kind of dried-out, uptight, neurotic man-hater she is. How could you do that to me, Pete?"

I desperately press my one line of attack. "If you're not everything she thinks you are, why were you playing FBI agent in my closet?"

FBI. She looks guilty now. She's an old civil rights buff, and whatever evidence she found against me, she found it without a warrant. "I didn't go snooping, Pete. It was Ofelia saw the edge of some chiffon sticking out of that bag. She was vacuuming the closet because you told her to stop missing corners."

That lousy peon. I took her on as sleep-in help because she settled for pay far under scale and so was

the thriftiest of all status symbols to show the jealous.
If I had this meddling status symbol in front of me
right now, I could kill her with my bare hands. I say
to Joan, "And then you had to rip apart that valise?
You couldn't simply ask me about it?"

"My God, is that the only thing on your mind?
How I found out? With everything going to pieces
around us?"

Divorce. There is a smell of divorce in the way she
says that. A smell of good-bye, Nick. See what happens, Nick, when you have such a smart mamma?
Somebody who reads all the books and knows all the
answers? Hell, if my mother ever turned up the
same goods on my father, the same dainties stained
with come and smeared with lipstick, she'd never figure out the answer in a dozen lifetimes. She wouldn't
believe the answer if he swore to it. She wouldn't even
believe it of one of those degenerate, long-haired hip-
pies she's always writing letters about to the *Miami
Herald*.

But not your mamma, Nick. For almost all her
married life your mamma has been handed sex on a
silver platter. Everything that can be done to tickle
those erogenous zones has been done to her, because,
let it be said without false modesty, your daddy when
turned on is quite the lover boy. And Mamma is one
of those cuties—one of that happy minority of females according to Dr. Kinsey—who digs pornogra-
phy, whether it comes under the heading of science or
smut. So, what with one thing and another, Mamma
knows all there is to know on the subject.

Just the same, Nick, bear in mind that as a woman
can use hysterical self-righteousness to win a battle, a
man can become Little Boy Lost to the same end.
Women are all mothers at heart, Nick, every fucking
one of them. Including those viragos who call themselves Women's Lib. And what each and every one of
them wants more than anything on earth is to have
the male animal standing there before her, thumb in

mouth, shit-kicking expression on his craggy face,
hopefully waiting for the motherly pat on the head
she's aching to give him.

I become Little Boy Lost. I become bruised and
beaten and prayerful. "Joanie, things don't have to go
to pieces. I don't want them to. I can't let them. For
God's sake, Joanie, help me."

She can't seem to make up her mind whether to
burst into tears or puke. "Pete, all this time that you
didn't tell me—didn't trust me—"

"These last few crazy months. That's all it's been."

"Oh, Pete." She settles for tears. A flood of them. I
go to her. She accepts my consolation, face wetly
against my shirt front, arms tightly around me, nails
digging into my back. She raises her face, alight with
the dawn of a new day. "Pete, it's no crime to have a
kinky streak get out of hand. And someone like Dr.
Ernst can help. I know how you feel about psychotherapy, but don't say no, Pete, don't get uptight about
it. I want to call him right now."

An ultimatum?

"Joanie, look—"

"I want to call him right now, Pete."

It's an ultimatum all right.

"Call him, Joanie. Tell him I want to see him as
soon as possible."

And whatever you do, don't stand too close to that
open window eight stories above East 60th Street
while you're dialing, dear, because, baby, you'd be
asking for it.

"Poor Peterkin." Herr Doktor is kittenishly sympathetic. "Was this confrontation with yourself so hard to take? Is the enlightenment so painful?"

The stunted son of a bitch knows it is. I am, as he has been working to make me, one painful mess. But I'll be damned if I give him the satisfaction of hearing it from me. I shrug indifferently—it costs another jolt of pain, that small motion of the shoulders—and he nods approval. Whether approval of my feigned indifference or of my stoicism, I don't know.

He turns to Joan. "As for you, dear child, this scene the defendant just presented to us—you can testify you found no distortions in it? No omissions?"

"No. But it winds up with me looking like a damn fool. Completely gullible. I wasn't all that gullible."

"You felt at the time that he was not being completely open?"

"Yes. So I made him tell me everything."

The doctor looks impressed. "His entire case history? From childhood?"

"No. Starting with when he became terrified because he couldn't make it with me any more. He said that's what led him to pick up a girl in London just to test himself, and the same thing happened with her. Until, kidding around with him, she put her wig on him, and he found it turned him on. Now he was really in a panic. So in Copenhagen he took up with another girl—"

"Her name was Karen?"

"I think so. Yes. Anyhow, this time he couldn't perform until he dressed up in her clothes."

"So. And did he also describe his relationship with a woman named Vivien Papazor?

"Yes. And how he carried out a whole elaborate scheme to get her lingerie back to our apartment. He said he was really trying to work up enough nerve to ask me to, well, go along with his kinky streak so maybe we could put our sex life together again. To let him wear those things when we made love and were alone in the house. He said it might still be the answer. At least, temporarily."

"And you accepted everything he said at face value?"

"At the time, yes. But I still couldn't see it his way." Joan's voice is taking on that familiar note of tearful despair. "I just couldn't. I mean, it might work for him, but it would work just the opposite for me. Turn me off completely. It was just too sick. I couldn't go along with it."

"He resigned himself to this?"

"He had to. I told him as long as he stayed in therapy and tried to straighten himself out, I'd be willing to make the best of it. I told him that the only alternative was divorce, and on my terms."

"Which were?"

"He'd never be allowed to see Nick again."

The hotel room smells of mildew. The chandelier casts a dim yellowish light from its one serviceable bulb over faded wallpaper and shabby furniture. The window offers a view of a grimy brick wall.

Vivien surveys this desolation smilingly. She softly sings: " 'New York, New York, it's a wonderful town—' "

"I'm sorry, Viv, but the place has to be off the beaten track."

"Well, we can't get much further off the beaten track, can we? Indoor plumbing, I trust? Or is there a potty under the bed?"

"No, the bathroom door is over there. Believe it or

not, dear, even a hole in the wall like this costs an arm and a leg. And on a long-term rental at that."

"If you're not going to atone for your sins, sir, the least you can do is pay for them. Now consider the Plaza—"

"I'll be brutally honest, Viv. This place'll do well enough for quickies, and you know that's all there can be for us. A couple of hours grabbed out of the working day now and then."

"Then lucky for you that I'm one of those depraved people who think furtive is fun. But you are being kept on a short leash, aren't you?"

"I can't take any chances, not with Nick at stake."

"I'm not complaining, darling. After all, if your wife was willing to play this game with you, where would that leave me?"

"Right where you are. Believe me, she could never play the game your way. She'd be so damn self-conscious and self-sacrificing about it, it would be miserable for both of us."

"And it isn't now?"

"It's not as bad as it might be. As long as I dutifully report to my shrink on schedule and make an occasional effort to service her, she seems content."

"And you?"

"I survive." I rest my hands on the swell of her hips. "Why not? Look what I've got for consolation."

"But not much time for it." She draws away, goes to the dresser, opens it. She fingers through the familiar lingerie. "All here?"

"All there."

"Loverly." When we had come into the room she had placed the parcel she was carrying on top of the dresser. She tears open its wrapping now, lifts the cover off a cardboard box. "And to add to the ensemble—" She holds up a wig and a pair of high-heeled slippers. "Now close those drapes, darling."

The blank wall outside the window is a guarantee that no one can possibly see us through that dirt-encrusted glass, but I know her foibles too well now to argue the point. I close the drapes.

"Furtive is fun," Irwin Gold says. "Sheesh."

"One of the basic tenets of Puritanism, Counselor," the doctor says. He shows his yellow fangs in a broad smile. "And considering the fortunes made from it by the enterprising, let us not deride it." He turns the smile on me. "Do you admit, Peterkin, that this bittersweet little scene just shown us is accurate in all details?"

"Yes."

"And such scenes were frequently repeated thereafter in those unappetizing quarters?"

"Yes."

"For how long a period?"

I'm willing to answer, but I can't. The pain of the ulcer is too much of a distraction, and the numbness in my legs and lower back from being held rigid in my chair seems to be possessing my brain.

The doctor's smile vanishes. "For how long afterward?"

"I don't know. I can't remember."

"So? But you must, furtive Peterkin. You must."

McMANUS CHEWS ON HIS CIGAR, studies his cards. He flips the deuce of hearts on the table, Joan covers with the nine, he overtakes with my ten from dummy, and Grace discards. Once or twice a month I am invited by McManus—ordered by him—to have him and a companion over for an evening of bridge, and Grace is the latest in a long line of companions, all members of McManus' bridge club, all chic, hard-faced tigresses who play at tournament level and would cut a throat for a master point. Hard on Joan, who has to partner the tigress of the moment since McManus won't play against a husband-and-wife team— *"For Christ's sake, a woman scratches her nose and her husband can tell her whole hand"*—but harder on me, who must be his permanent partner at these sessions. Bluff, hearty Jekyll at the dinner table for the benefit of the ladies, he becomes super-Hyde as soon as the cards are dealt.

Now as he reaches out, plucks the six of diamonds from dummy, I can only pray that his luck in squeezing out extra tricks tonight has finally gone sour on him. No chance. Grace drops the five of diamonds, McManus discards a losing heart from his hand, Joan discards, and McManus hauls in the trick. He gives me a poisonous look before I can avoid his eye, reaches out, plays the thirteenth diamond from dummy, discards his only other loser, and lays down the remaining cards in his hand. "All the rest trump. Twelve tricks in spades."

Grace pulls over the score pad, picks up the pencil.

"That's game," she says, and then, bitch that she is, can't resist saying, "and a very pretty slam. But not bid."

"Did you hear that?" McManus says to me. "Or should she say it again?"

"Charlie, we did not have a slam setup."

"Obviously we did, because we made slam, didn't we?"

"I do not bid on wild hopes, Charlie. I bid the cards I hold."

His face is actually going livid, his neck swelling. "Don't give me that fucking line. I was gunning for slam, and you knew it. And still you stopped the bidding dead."

"If you were holding my cards—"

"I said don't give me that shit. Just for once admit you were wrong, that's all. Admit you don't know the first goddam thing about this game."

"I'll do better than that." He has gotten me to where I almost rip my pocket apart digging my hand in it for my money clip. "I cost us five hundred points? Here's the five dollars. And from now on we'll skip the loud post-mortems, and I'll just pay you whatever you think my bidding costs you. It'll be worth it."

"Pay me with my own money?" Out of long and bitter experience I recognize that deadly tone. He is laying aside the shillelagh now, picking up the carving knife, testing its blade with his thumb. "You are going to put me in my place with my own money?"

"My money, Charlie." I drop the five-dollar bill in the middle of the table. Let him take it or not as he chooses. "Like this."

"Oh, Jesus Christ," Joan says. "These merry post-mortems. How about playing cards?"

McManus is deaf to her. He leans toward me. He pokes his thumb into his chest. "My money, Jack. Because that's what the accountant came crying to me about yesterday. Room three-ten at the Hotel Criterion. Ten months' rent at three hundred bucks a month. Three thousand dollars of my money. You know goddam well I never yet made an issue of anything you put down on the expense sheet, but between those deadhead geniuses you planted on me and your fucking generosity with my money right now, this one really sticks in the throat!"

"Charlie, that hotel bill—"

"Yeah, what about it? Are you going to have the gall to sit there and tell me you used a fleabag like that for company business?"

Joan abruptly gets to her feet and walks out of the room. I hear the swinging door to the kitchen slam against the edge of the stove. I stand and look down at McManus. "Pretty good at bridge, but a real champ at dirty pool, aren't you, Charlie?"

For once, no answer. What the hell answer is there?

Joan is standing at the kitchen table, her clenched hands resting on the table, her head down.

"Joan, listen to me. Before this gets out of hand, I want you to understand that I have been using that room for company business and only company business. You know what Charlie is like. It's a pressure cooker in the goddam office when he's there. The only solution I could think of was to take a room around there and clear up what work I could in private. It would be worth it even if it came out of my own pocket. That is the God's honest truth, Joan."

She raises her head. "I want to see that room now. Just get rid of them. Then we're going to that hotel."

"At one in the morning? For no reason? Look, Joan, the first thing tomorrow morning—"

"Now. With you or without you, I am going to see that room now."

"And what the hell do you think you'll find there? Or is it who do you think you'll find there?"

"I'll find whatever you left there. My God, you're sick. You are sick. And you don't want to do anything about it. You never tried to do anything about it all this time."

North, south, east, and west, the gates slam shut. "Joanie, I have been trying. Jesus Christ, psychic compulsions aren't something you just wish away. You know that. With a little more time—"

"No. Tomorrow, Nick and I will move in with the folks. Monday, I'll see a lawyer about the divorce."

"Do you have any idea what it'll do to Nick if you walk out like that?"

"Do you have any idea what you've just done to me?"

"Look. He needs time. He needs some preparation. We can let him know we're breaking up while we're still all together. He deserves that much consideration, Joan. One lousy week."

She says in a voice of exhaustion. "A week. And then I tell him it's final."

"I'll tell him. You don't have to worry. I'll do it with proper restraint."

"And with the understanding that this is good-bye for good."

"Oh no."

She says incredulously, "Do you think for one minute I'd let you—" She doesn't finish it. If she has a finish for it, she can't find the words to put it in.

"Let me what? You know damn well what I've got isn't catching." I walk over to her, take both her wrists in one hand, get them in a tight grip. "Let's get it straight right now. If you try to cut me out of visitation rights, I will not be responsible for what happens. We all have a breaking point, dear, and that is mine. As far as I'm concerned, my son is what it's all about. Cut him out of my life—even give him the slightest reason for wanting to be cut out of my life—and you are putting your own neck right on the chopping block. Understand?"

I grip her wrists tighter and she makes a face of anguish. "Pete, let go. You're hurting me."

I ease up on my grip. "Now I think you've got the idea," I say.

"So THERE IT IS, your honor," Gold says with satisfaction. "The complete wrap-up."

"Is it?"

Gold ticks it off on his fingers. "That scene shows he's ready to commit violence against anyone who gets between him and his son. Now, two years after the divorce, he's cooled off on Vivien and recognizes she's the one broke up his home. And today when he goes home early to wait for his son, he finds Vivien already there, looking for action. Who could have let her in? Only the maid. If the maid talks, it means real trouble with his ex-wife. She'd have every right now to keep the boy completely away from him. He has this out with Vivien, he boils over, he shoots her. As I said, a complete wrap-up."

The doctor looks at me. "Do you find anything to challenge in this summation?"

"No."

"You may not have noticed, Peterkin, but one member of the jury has not yet been heard."

"Nobody else has to be heard. The way Gold explained it was the way it happened."

"You are the one who selected the jury, Peterkin. By the rules of this court, every member of it must be heard."

"Another rule you just cooked up? God damn it, I told you nobody else has to be heard. I don't want to hear any more."

He disregards me. He points at the far end of that row of motionless, glassy-eyed figures. "You, young lady."

She pats my father's cheek, detaches herself from him, lazily gets to her feet. She is tall, redheaded, snub-nosed, blue-eyed, her lips glistening with bright red lipstick, her eyebrows thin black lines. The red hair is caught up in a snood. She is very young, a big, curvy, baby-faced girl. "Yes, Judge?" There is a touch of Yankee twang in the voice as well as a hint of Confederate drawl. You have to be born and raised in South Florida to recognize that mixture offhand. The Dade County redneck mixture.

The doctor says, "Your name, young lady?"

She nods toward me. There is enormous contempt in the gesture. "He likes it to be Vivien, Judge. Same as that one in *Gone With the Wind*. She was the one gave him his first real hots. I guess I was next."

"You know the defendant well?"

"I was with him maybe ten minutes when he was a kid down in Miami, so how well could it be? But it looks like he never did get me out of his twisty little mind, did he? Because he's a jack-off artist, Judge, see? And I'm the dream girl he wants for company, comes jack-off times."

"Then the name Papazor—"

"That is no name, Judge. That is what his bigmouth sister told him I was, first time he ever got a look at me right there on Flagler Street."

Right there on Flagler Street. All ass and legs. My sister put her mouth to my ear and whispered it. "That's Papa's whore!"

Vivien, Papa's whore.

Vivien Papazor.

I glare at her across the room. "You're lying. She's dead. I killed her. You know I killed her."

She spits the words at me. "Jack-off artist! Now you know what you are, don't you? A fucking useless jack-off artist!"

"No!" Suddenly the room, everyone in it, is liquefying, running together into a puddle of distorted shapes, blinding colors.

"Wait!" I shout.

THE BATHROOM.

The bloody, bloody bathroom.

Myself draped over the hamper like a dead buck draped over a car fender. Myself facing myself in the full-length mirror on the door. Blearily. One-eyed. When I fell the wig was jolted out of place and strands of it cover the other eye. But I can see that the string of blood along the mirrored reflection of my jaw has widened now into a ribbon, the drip of it down the side of the hamper is a little faster.

Eli, Eli lama sabacthani. Hit a bull's eye with a handgun five out of five at twenty yards. Miss it with the gun thrust against the target.

I have frozen with my finger on the trigger of a gun only once in my life.

I shoved the barrel of the revolver into my mouth like a swabstick and held it there, the front sight digging into my palate. And still held it there, my finger paralyzed on the trigger. God damn it, if I pulled the trigger, I wouldn't even feel the impact of the bullet against my brain. But I can't. Ernie Hemingway could do it with a shotgun; I can't even do it with a .38. But it must be done. All right, take it out, barrel wet with saliva, press it to the heart. Squeeze the trigger. Jesus Christ, it's like a white-hot bolt driven through the chest.

Dead? Not yet. Just slowly, slowly dying. Tough specimen. Same as that eight-pointer you dropped dead with a single shot right on the mark. Except that it lay twitching until you had Nick cut its throat. His first. His blooding. Green around the gills.

"Feeling queasy, Nick?"

"Some. But it's all right. I guess I'm supposed to, first time out."

Twelve years old then, and cool, man, cool.

Friday.

Good Friday.

Godforsaken Friday.

Breakfast. Half a cup of black coffee, half a cigarette, three capsules. *Methamphetamine hydrochloric as prescribed.* Ups to shift the gears that downs had put in reverse during the night. Ofelia hauling the vacuum cleaner out of the closet, standing there studying the button in the handle. Ten years, and she still wonders what will happen when she pushes that little button.

Joan had said in the lawyer's office, "Another thing. I want Ofelia there whenever Nick is there. Every weekend, Friday through Sunday."

She didn't have to draw a diagram for me. "You mean she'll be house-mother? She'll protect my son from me? The hell with that."

Irwin Gold had said. "He may be right, Mrs. Hibben. Now why not let's compromise with her going there Fridays?"

He may be right, Mrs. Hibben. Why waste time picking over the small print, Mrs. Hibben, when you and I could go up to my place right now and knock off a piece? I'm small but wiry, baby. Not long, but strong.

Three capsules.

We all have our fantasies. Lenny Bruce fantasized that mainlining speed gave it more bounce to the ounce. Wrong. What he really liked was the strap around the arm, the needle, the image of the bad boy ramming it up the asshole of respectability. A wrecker. Knock everything down and plant a phallus on the rubble to worship. Circumcised, of course.

I turned Nick off Liverlips Lenny. He bought a couple of the records, was playing them to death, memorizing them. I told him about the pale, fat, self-righteous slug from under the rock who mainlined himself to death in a puddle of vomit. "The point is, Nick, you don't have to admire what a Bob Hope stands for to despise what a Lenny Bruce stands for." The perfect way to put it. Another phase ended. No more of those records around the apartment.

Three capsules. The ignition takes hold on my way to the office. The motor is in high even before I'm at my desk.

Good Friday.

Sweaty Friday for the Catholics in the office. An optional holiday for them. But cutbacks in personnel have them pissing in their didies. Which way to go to make Charles McManus, Knight of Columbus, happy? Stay away and show how much you love the Pope, or sign in and show how much you love the job? Once, most of them stayed away. Today, most of them seem to be here. Let the Pope worry.

Pope Julius. Grandpa Julius, the saint of Upper Broadway. Joan said, "If it's a boy, we can name him Julian." I said, "He's due Christmas Week. We'll name him Nicholas." He was named Nicholas Julian. He never signed Julian on any school paper. He was circumcised but not bar-mitzvahed. He attended synagogue with his grandpa for one hour every Yom Kippur, but he assured me that Zen had all the answers. He shopped for his grandma when he went across town to visit, carting brown paper bags of groceries through the streets for her like a nice Yiddisher grandson, but at fourteen he could throw a football forty yards in a perfect spiral and land it on a dime. You lose some, you win some.

My secretary had the coffee ready for me, this time with milk and sugar in it. Miss Golliwog, the latest of a series of secretarial disasters. A dusky maiden, out of Harlem by Mischance, winner of the Useless

Sweepstakes. Fucking Afro hairdo blocks out half the room when she stands there. A wig? Ask her and you've violated the First, Fifth, and Fourteenth Amendments.

"Mr. McManus wanted to see you as soon as you came in, Mr. Hibben."

That prissy voice. I have good news and I have bad news. The good news is that three capsules will vividly heighten perception. Oh, but heighten it. The bad news is that heightened perception means watching those secretarial lips slowly shape each syllable, means hearing each rounded syllable in all its fruity beauty. An experience to turn the strongest stomach.

"Thank you, Miss Golliwog." And then the devil made me do it. "Is that a wig, by any chance?"

The lips writhed into action again. "Yes it is, Mr. Hibben." Smiling. Because now she has a case for the Supreme Court.

McManus sunk down in that monstrous chair behind that monstrous desk. Pint-sized, jowly, looked unshaven. But then he looked unshaven even after a shave. And that stinking cigar first thing in the morning. Good old Charlie, America's most undesirable bachelor.

"You feeling all right, Pete?"

"Fine."

"You don't look it. You look like hell."

"Charlie, I've got a pile of work to clear up. Let's skip the medical examination."

"Sure." He studied the cigar. Some day, some incredible day, he is going to come out with it and apologize for blowing my marriage apart. Today? No. "Any orders in that pile for six thousand sets of Grondahl? One hundred and twenty thousand copies at two dollars' production cost per copy?"

"They're moving."

"Moving, shit. Your grandchildren won't live long enough to see them cleared out of the warehouse."

"Charlie, we've been through this a dozen times.

It's a long-term investment. Sooner or later, we'll pass the break-even point on it."

"Yeah? Or is it you're thinking that when Vince's new one comes in it'll wash out some of that red ink we're floating on?"

I didn't like the way he said that. "Don't tell me you're worried that the new one'll be a dud. You know better than that, Charlie."

"Uh-huh. I also know Vince and Betsy had me over for dinner last night. And do you know what came with the dessert?"

"What?"

"Some interesting news. Vince wants out. We don't get the new one. Or any other."

Thank God for those three capsules. But even with them peaking in me, I am rocked back on my heels. "I don't understand, Charlie. Vince must be out of his mind. Why does he want out? What the hell's gotten into him?"

"Oh, that. Seems he's unhappy, Pete. Seems you worry a lot more about your prize-winning pets than you do about him. So you'd better get to him fast and try to make him happy again. He needs love, Pete. Moneymakers need love the same as geniuses. So now you show him just how much love you can give him, right up to kissing his ass in Brentano's window. Or else."

Or else.

I sat at my desk getting a rough ride from the capsules. I went home at noon. The hell with coming back today.

No Ofelia. A note on the phone pad. Big block letters in a raggedy row spelling out *noscool sonic comic loc*. That was it. A message easy to decipher if I was in a mood to hunt up my decoder ring, which I was not.

At least three hours before Nick would show up from school. Three empty, inviting hours.

Horny time in a hot bath. Tension-relieving time.

Soaping the tool, I almost blew off, but none of that, Jack. Better things lie ahead. Lie abed. Toweled off, sweet-scented as a baby's bottom, I went into the bedroom.

Four valises on the top shelf now. Two for lingerie, one for wigs, one for shoes. I took my time selecting. The clock said one, Nick would not show up until three-thirty. Still plenty of time left for Vivien.

What about Offenbach and Orff as a team, Viv? Costume suggested by Offenbach, music by Orff.

Tummy-tightening and titillating, my pet. A cancan girl being humped to the beat of *Carmina Burana*. Inspired, pet. And now bring that stereo volume up. Louder. And louder. Let's swim in that sound.

Finally the shoes and the wig. The shoulder-length raven-haired wig. The eyelashes. Remember how tricky it was at first with the eyelashes? The make-up. Now look at that. Look as close in the glass as you want to. A fucking work of art if I say so myself.

Tool in hand, hand pumping in voluptuous slow motion, look close.

Look at Nick.

Nick?

I wheeled around. He stood there in the doorway, staring. Eyes huge, face sheet-white, drained of all blood. Shock. The real thing. Ready to black out.

He didn't. He made it as far as the armchair in the living room, hung over the chair, ready to heave up on it.

The two guns in their holsters in the bottom drawer of the dresser. He never saw me come up behind him, never heard me through that roar from the stereo. Six inches away. One shot centered in back of the skull.

He never knew. He was, then he wasn't. Not an instant of pain in the going. Not a microsecond.

I didn't look. I went into the bathroom, closed the door, thrust the barrel into my mouth, tried to squeeze the trigger, tried, tried, then pressed the muzzle into my chest and squeezed.

Silence.

Carmina Burana is ended.

And when the expanding numbness in my arms and legs reaches this flaming bolt in my chest and extinguishes the flame, I am ended too.

Slowly, wearily, painfully done for. *Spurlos versenkt.*

Listen to me, Nick.

Nick, listen to me.

It had to be both of us. I couldn't let you try to live with what you knew, because you weren't meant to live despising me. And I wasn't meant to live without you. So it was an act of love. A final, total act of love. It had to be. Otherwise it wouldn't make any sense, would it?

What doesn't make sense, what makes it look like a terrible joke played on us, Nick, is that it happened only because you walked in at the wrong time. You came too early. And without warning. If you had only phoned the apartment, had left a message—

The note on the phone pad! But I didn't have time to decipher it while Vivien was waiting.

noscool sonic comic loc

Friday. But Good Friday. A holiday.

no school so nic come l cloc

Oh God almighty, Ofelia, you wreaker of disaster, you miserable, fucking nemesis, what did he say to you over the phone?

Wasn't it, *If Father calls, tell him there's no school today, so I'll be over at one o'clock?*

Wasn't it, Ofelia?

WASN'T IT!

BESTSELLERS
FROM DELL

fiction